BBC
DOCTOR WHO

Time Lord
Quiz
Quest

PUFFIN

Hello, I'm the Doctor.

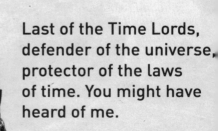

Last of the Time Lords, defender of the universe, protector of the laws of time. You might have heard of me.

In the never-ending fight against the darkness I need allies, friends, companions. But how handy are you in a crisis? Do you know one end of a sonic screwdriver from the other? Think you could pilot the TARDIS in an emergency? Can you tell your Silurians from your Slitheen? Your Ogri from your Ogrons?

From Autons to Zygons, you're going to meet them all. And you're going to need to be able to work out how to escape from any tricky situation.

Are you up to the challenge? (Although, obviously, being human you're automatically at a disadvantage.) Can you think your way out of trouble, or are you about as imaginative as a Dalek? (And I'm not talking about my unusual pal Rusty here.)

Are you a Time Lord in training, or will I be forced to unleash the attack eyebrows in a frown of fury at your staggering stupidity? In other words, will you be joining me on my travels through all of time and space, or will you be crowned ruler of the Planet of the Pudding Brains?

CONTENTS

TRUE TIME LORD

NEWLY REGENERATED

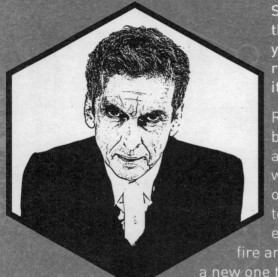

So here we are, at the beginning of your journey. Newly regenerated, as it were . . .

Regeneration. It's both a blessing and a curse. One body gets worn out, irradiated or dropped off a radio telescope, there's an eruption of golden fire and suddenly I've got a new one to start all over again in. It's like putting on a clean shirt. Everything's hunky-dory. At least, it is in the end. Thing is, I never know where the faces come from. But that's enough about me – let's get back to you.

We need to break you in gently with some questions that even the inhabitants of Planet Pudding Brain could answer.

But be careful – you're going to need to use your eyes as well as your brain. And your fingers, for adding up on. **Probably.**

The Regeneration Game

To get you started, tell me: which words were the ones that each of my new faces said first? Simply match the first words to the faces.

'You were expecting someone else?'

'Legs! Still got legs, good!! Arms, hands. Ooh, fingers. Lots of fingers. '

'Typical Sontaran attitude . . . stop Linx . . . perverting the course of human history . . .'

'Hello! OK – oh. New teeth. That's weird. So, where was I? Oh, that's right. Barcelona!'

'Slower! Slower! Concentrate on one thing. One thing!'

'Kidneys! I've got new kidneys! I don't like the colour.'

'Oh no, Mel.'

'I . . . Oh . . .'

'Shoes. Must find my shoes.'

'Who am I? Who am I?'

Trenzalore Test

So you fancy yourself potential Time Lord material, do you? Well, if you're going to travel with me, you're going to need to know where I came from, so to speak.

Before I last regenerated, I spent 900 years protecting the planet Trenzalore from being attacked by some of the deadliest species in the universe. But how much do you know about my time on Trenzalore?

1 What was the name of the village I protected on Trenzalore?

A   Christmas

B   Easter

C   Leadworth

2 My enemies were drawn to Trenzalore by a mysterious message that echoed out across the stars, but what was the message and where was it sent from?

A   A global phone call, sent from the stolen Earth

B   The First Question, sent from Gallifrey

C   'Dinner's ready', sent from Clara's flat

3 The Papal Mainframe arrived at Trenzalore first, creating a force field round the planet to protect the village. But which race had already arrived and was hidden in the snow?

A   The Ice Warriors

B   The Snowmen

C   The Weeping Angels

4 Who was the Mother Superious of the Papal Mainframe, and an old friend of mine to boot?

A   River Song

B   Tasha Lem

C   Amy Pond

5 The Mother Superious changed the faith of the Papal Mainframe into the Church of what, to stop me from saying my name?

A   The Church of Daleks

B   The Church of Gallifrey

C   The Church of the Silence

6 During my first 300 years on Trenzalore, who was my only companion?

A   Clara Oswald

B   The TARDIS

C   Handles

7 My enemies wanted me to answer the First Question, but if I had who would it have brought back, causing the Last Great Time War to start again?

A   The Time Lords

B   Rose Tyler

C   The War Doctor

8 Each of my ancient enemies tried various ways of penetrating the force field round the village, but what did the Cybermen use?

A   A wooden Cyberman

B   A golden Cyberman

C   A Cybus Cyberman

9 The Daleks turned their attention to the Church itself. What did they do after assaulting the Mainframe?

A   They vaporised everyone

B   They turned everyone into Dalek puppets

C   They attacked the other alien fleets in orbit around the planet

10 Who did I later ally myself with to repel Dalek attacks on Trenzalore?

A   The Ice Warriors

B   The Sontarans

C   The Silents

11 Dying of old age, having reached the end of my regeneration cycle, I prepared to sacrifice myself to the Daleks until what happened?

A   The Daleks left Trenzalore

B   The crack in space and time closed

C   The Time Lords granted me a new regeneration cycle

12 Where did I make my final stand on Trenzalore?

A   Inside the TARDIS

B   At the top of the village clock tower

C   On board the Dalek saucer

13 Where was Clara for most of the time I was living on Trenzalore?

A   Having Christmas dinner with her family

B   Aboard the Papal Mainframe

C   Trapped at the centre of the TARDIS

The Game Is Afoot

Do you remember when I ran into a bit of bother with the Half-Face Man in Victorian London? Well, imagine you are the Great Detective Madame Vastra. You have to keep the robot under observation and stop the dinosaur leaving the Thames.

Place one T-Rex, one Half-Face Man, one Paternoster Gang member and one sonic shield in each of the empty squares in the grid, so that every row, every column and every two-by-two box contains one of each type. Go!

Paternoster Gang member	Half-Face Man	T-Rex	Sonic Shield
Half-Face Man	Sonic Shield	Paternoster Gang member	T-Rex

Puzzling Pairs

Observation – that's the name of the game. If you're going to be of any use to anyone, it's all about what you can spot, no matter how small the differences.

Take a look at these images. Each pair is identical, right? Wrong! Only one pair actually matches, but which one is it?

Alien Alliance

I'm always getting blamed for things I haven't done –
or at least that I haven't done yet.

For example, some of my enemies once
formed an alliance to stop the greatest
threat in the universe: me! The cheek
of it!

The names of some of those races
are hidden in the wordsearch
below. The question is: can you
find them?

- Atraxi
- Autons
- Blowfish
- Cybermen
- Daleks
- Draconians
- Drahvins
- Haemogoth
- Hoix
- Judoon
- Silurians
- Slitheen
- Sontarans
- Sycorax
- Terileptils
- Uvodni
- Weevils
- Zygons

```
H R S J H I O S C N W G U N H
U S A Y N O N W A E E D U O A
F U I D C I I T B M E A V O E
Q R O F V O R X T R V B V D M
R V O H W A R Q I E I U P U O
U D A I X O V A S B L T L J G
X R R I D D L I X Y S W H N O
D S D A W V L B W C N G J O T
S X B G C U S L I T H E E N H
C K U D R O S N A R A T N O S
C P E I M S N O T U A W T J N
Y H A L T E R I L E P T I L S
T N K B A O E Q A Z Y G O N S
S G Q G S D E P N N V S S Z H
B S H U P I Y I M G S V Y E B
```

The TARDIS – A Beginner's Guide

You think you know me? You think you *really* know who the Doctor is? Let's test that out, shall we? We'll start with some simple questions about my time machine, the TARDIS.

For example, do you know what the TARDIS was called when she became temporarily humanoid? Ha! That's foxed you, hasn't it? Well, come on. Didn't they teach you anything at Stupid School?

Circle the answer you believe to be correct in each case on the next few pages . . .

1 Let's start with the basics. What does the acronym TARDIS stand for?

Time And Relative Dimension In Space

Tiny And Radically Different InSide

 2 That one was too easy, wasn't it? But how about this: what model is my TARDIS?

Paradox Machine

Type 40 TT Capsule

 3 What device is it that enables a TARDIS to change its outward appearance, but which is jammed in my TARDIS?

The Chameleon Arch

The Chameleon Circuit

4 What does the exterior of the TARDIS appear to be made of?

Wood

Dalekanium

5 How many people are supposed to pilot the TARDIS?

Six

Two

6 What is the central column that rises from the TARDIS console?

The Heart of the TARDIS

The Time Rotor

7 From time to time, what device for storing headgear and protective outer garments with long sleeves have I kept in the console room?

A Genesis Ark

A hatstand

8 A recreation of which famous ship once crashed through the walls of the TARDIS after I deactivated the old girl's force fields?

The SS *Titanic*

The SS *Great Britain*

9 When the TARDIS crash-landed in Amelia Pond's back garden in Leadworth, where did I end up?

In the swimming pool

In the library

10 Anyway, you haven't answered my original question yet. (No, not the one about Stupid School.) What name did the TARDIS go by when her matrix was transferred into a humanoid body?

Susan

Idris

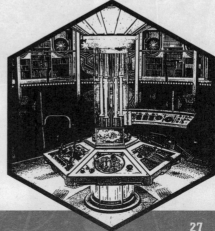

The Paternoster Gang

If you're going to travel with me you need to know who you can trust if things ever go a bit . . . iffy. Take the Paternoster Gang, for example. How much do you know about that bunch of troublemakers?

Use the words listed here to fill in the blanks in the passage on the next page.

Sweetville

Demons Run

snow

Paternoster Row

Crimson Horror

Red Leech

Great Intelligence

Trenzalore

Silurian

The Paternoster Gang is a group of detectives active in Victorian London that is named after _____, the street on which their headquarters are located. The gang includes Madame Vastra, who is a _____, Jenny Flint and Strax. All of them aided me during the Battle of _____.

On Christmas Eve, 1893, the gang also helped me to stop the _____ from taking over the Earth by using telepathic _____.

During the Case of the _____, a man called Mr Thursday asked Vastra to investigate the murder of his brother, which led the gang to _____. There they put an end to Winifred Gillyflower's plan to wipe out humanity using _____ poison.

They also travelled with me to _____, where they entered my tomb in order to battle the Great Intelligence once again.

Repurpose, Repair, Repeat

Robots repairing themselves – that was what Clara and I encountered in Victorian London. It wasn't the first time I'd seen something like that, and it wasn't my first run-in with automatons either.

Take a look at these individuals who liked rebuilding themselves (from bits of other people, usually). Can you match them with their missing pieces?

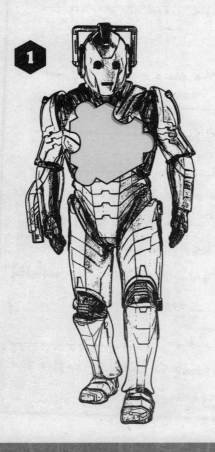

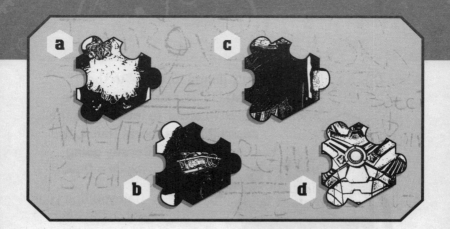

Into the Dalek

When Clara and I temporarily joined forces with the Combined Galactic Resistance, we were miniaturised in order to investigate the possibility of a moral Dalek, by literally going *inside* a Dalek!

Can you find your way to the heart of the labyrinth and the monster that lurks within? And, more importantly, can you find your way back out again?

FINISH

Dalek Deductions

The Daleks have to be among my most determined enemies. No matter how many times I defeat them, they keep coming back for more.

But how much do you know about these genetically engineered mutants, which belong to fundamental DNA type 467-989 and are originally from a planet in the Seventh Galaxy?

Match the questions to the correct answers.

1 Who was the creator of the Daleks?

2 What is the Daleks' favourite, and most over-used, catchphrase?

3 What was the name given to the secret order of four Daleks that each had distinct personalities?

4 What was the name of the prison ship created by the Time Lords during the Last Great Time War to hold millions of Daleks prisoner?

5 What are the robotic guards located inside the Dalekanium casing of a Dalek called?

6 What nickname did I give to the damaged Dalek that had been captured by the Combined Galactic Resistance?

7 What was the name of the super-weapon created by the New Dalek Empire and powered by an engine formed from twenty-six planets and one moon in perfect alignment?

8 Who did I first encounter inside the Dalek Asylum that would later become one of my most faithful friends?

9 When I met the Daleks during World War Two, what did Winston Churchill call them?

10 What colour was the Dalek Supreme of the New Dalek Paradigm?

A Clara Oswald

B White

C Rusty

D Ironsides

E The Reality Bomb

F Davros

G Dalek Antibodies

H The Cult of Skaro

I The Genesis Ark

J 'Exterminate!'

Alien Museum

I thought I had wiped out the Daleks at the end of the Last Great Time War. So you can imagine how I felt when I discovered one in a museum of alien artefacts. But what else was hidden inside Henry van Statten's vault?

Identify the alien species by linking the name of each species to the correct museum piece.

Jagaroth

Slitheen

Cybermen

Ice Warriors

Silurians

Scarecrows

Escape From the Pandorica

You remember I was telling you about that time I was imprisoned inside the Pandorica by an alliance of my oldest enemies? I escaped, of course – but could you?

Start at the centre of the maze and see how long it takes you to negotiate the layers of deadlocks, time stops and matter lines in order to reach the outer edge.

Deadly Dinosaurs

Considering they died out sixty-five million years ago, dinosaurs have a terrible habit of turning up all over the place when you're least expecting it.

I've selected some of the strangest of these appearances. You have to work out which dino is which before fitting its name into the word grid. Here's a clue: two kinds of dinosaur appear twice in the grid.

DOWN

1 I brought this unlucky lady with me to Victorian London by accident. (4)

2 Tricey, who liked collecting golf balls, was one of these. A dino with big horns. (11)

3 These dinosaurs have pointy plates all down their backs. (11)

5 This flying dinosaur was in the Silurian Ark. (11)

ACROSS

2 I once found one of these gigantic dinos wandering in some caves. He had tiny arms. (4)

4 One of these herbivores terrorised London sixty-five million years after it became extinct. (11)

6 These dinosaurs are small, vicious and very, very speedy. (13)

The Impossible Girl

My friend Clara really can be impossible sometimes, but just *how* impossible? Or, to put it another way, how much do you know about the Impossible Girl?

4 After her adventures inside my tomb on Trenzalore, Clara became a _____. (7)

6 To help her remember the Wi-Fi password 'rycbar123', Clara came up with the phrase 'Run, you clever boy, and _____'. (8)

9 What was the name of the prison planet for insane Daleks where I first met Soufflé Girl? (5,6)

10 How did Victorian Clara describe the TARDIS the first time she saw it? 'It's _____ on the outside.' (7)

1 To save my life after encountering the Great Intelligence on Trenzalore, Clara threw herself into my _____. (8)

2 Clara used this thing from a tree to defeat the planet Akhaten. (4)

3 In 1892, Clara Oswin Oswald was working as a barmaid and a _____. (9)

5 Whilst trying to make our way to the centre of the TARDIS, Clara and I encountered a possible future form of herself. What was it? (4,6)

7 Who was Clara's boyfriend – the one I called 'P.E.'? (5,4)

8 I was living in a monastery in _____ when the Impossible Girl called me on the TARDIS phone. (7)

The Lonely Traveller

It has been said, more than once, that I shouldn't travel alone or be left to my own devices. As Clara put it once: 'I'm his carer.'

Over the centuries companions have come and gone, but how much do you know about my fellow time travellers?

1 My first companion was Susan. How were she and I related?

A Daughter and father

B Niece and uncle

C Granddaughter and grandfather

2 I met one of my most faithful companions, an investigative journalist, on Earth in the 1970s. I ran into her again many regenerations later in 2006. Who was she?

A Liz Shaw

B Jo Grant

C Sarah Jane Smith

3 Adric was a young mathematics genius, but he died trying to save the world. Which species was ultimately responsible for his death?

A The Cybermen

B The Daleks

C The Sontarans

4 What nationality was my former assistant Perpugilliam Brown, better known as Peri?

A American

B British

C Australian

5 What was the first thing I said to Rose Tyler when I met her in the basement of Henrik's, the department store where she worked?

A 'Hello!'

B 'Run!'

C 'Fantastic!'

6 What was Martha Jones training to be when I first met her?

A A solicitor

B A doctor

C A teacher

7 Where did Donna Noble and I first meet?

A Aboard the TARDIS

B At her wedding

C Adipose Industries

8 Donna's grandfather also once joined me on an adventure, which fulfilled a dark prophecy. What was his name?

A Geoff Noble

B Wilfred Noble

C Wilfred Mott

9 Aboard the interstellar cruise liner *Titanic* I met perhaps my greatest companion who never was, Astrid Peth. But what was Astrid doing on board the peculiar spaceship?

A She was a passenger

B She was a waitress

C She was a stowaway

10 Amelia Pond: the girl who waited. But how long did she have to wait for me to return when I took what I claimed would be a quick five-minute trip into the future?

A 6 months

B 12 years

C 36 years

11 Rory Williams, Amy's fiancé, didn't have an easy time of it travelling with me either. What was it that kept happening to him?

A He kept dying

B Soldiers kept invading his house when he wasn't wearing any trousers

C He kept turning into an Auton

12 Who has been my one constant companion throughout all my centuries of exploring the universe?

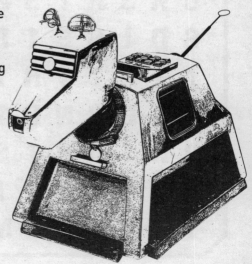

A K-9

B Clara

C The TARDIS

The Doctor's Wife

Once, in a bubble universe, the TARDIS had her matrix transferred into the body of a young woman called Idris.

Reuniting police box and matrix would be far too tricky for someone from the Planet of the Pudding Brains, but perhaps you can unpick this little teaser. How many times do the words TARDIS and IDRIS appear in the grid below?

```
I D R I S I D R A T S
B O T H I D R I S W I
O T A R D I S R I D D
S A F E R A I I D T R
U R S R I S R D R E A
S D I S S I D R A T T
I I R I I R I I T A A
D S D R N D T S R R R
R H I D R I S D E D D
A G R I I D I T E I I
T N S T I S M E S S S
```

Unusual Entities

I have run into all manner of malevolent entities over the centuries, but some were more monstrous than others. How much do you know about these unusual entities?

1 On one occasion, the gaseous predators known as the Family of Blood pursued me to a boarding school in England in 1913, tracking me using which sense?

A Sight

B Smell

C Hearing

2 Not long after meeting Rose Tyler, I ran afoul of the Nestene Consciousness. What material could its life force inhabit?

A Metal

B Plastic

C Flesh

3 The alien criminal known as the Wire stole the essences of the population of Great Britain whilst they were watching which televised event?

A The 1969 Moon Landing

B The 2012 London Olympics

C The Queen's Coronation in 1953

Spaceship Sequences

The robots that took over Nottingham Castle in the 12th century were busy casting circuits out of gold to repair their damaged spaceship.

Can you work out which piece is missing from each of the following circuits?

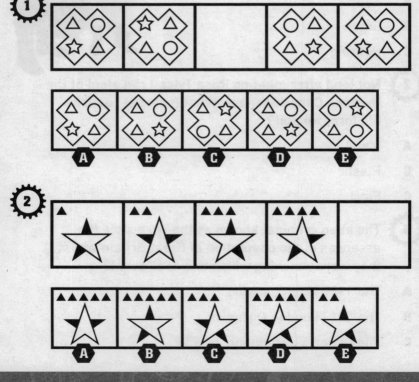

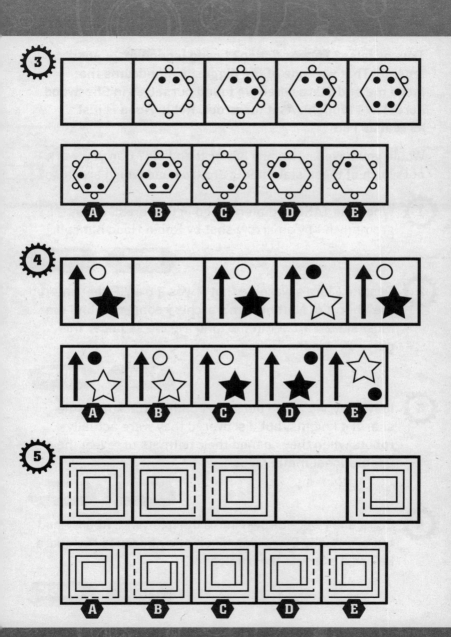

Riddles of Sherwood

True or false? Fact or fiction? Living legend or . . . just legend? That was one of the biggest conundrums that faced me and Clara when we found ourselves in Sherwood Forest in 1190(ish). As it turns out, Robin Hood is just as real as I am!

Would you have known any better than I did? Can you work out which of these statements are true and which are false?

1 When the TARDIS materialised in the forest, it was promptly hit by an arrow shot by Robin Hood himself.

TRUE   FALSE

2 Despite Clara's warning that it was a trap, Robin entered the Sheriff of Nottingham's archery contest to find the most skilled archer in the land. He did so under the guise of Tom the Tinker.

TRUE   FALSE

3 Inevitably, we found ourselves under attack from the sheriff's knights, but discovered they were actually robots when they opened their helmets to reveal their unemotional metal faces.

TRUE   FALSE

4 Clara and I were thrown into a dungeon with Robin Hood , but eventually Clara was taken away because the guard believed she was the ringleader.

TRUE   FALSE

5 Clara discovered that the sheriff had witnessed the robots' spaceship crashing and had been trying to repair it by collecting all the silver in the region to repair its damaged circuits.

TRUE   FALSE

6 Robin and I eventually escaped, ultimately finding ourselves in the spaceship inside the castle. The ship originated from the 37th century and its navigation computer was set to reach the Promised Land.

TRUE   FALSE

7 The robots launched their spaceship, but Robin fired the golden arrow from the archery contest into its engines to blow it up before it could leave Earth's atmosphere.

TRUE   FALSE

8 When we finally left Robin Hood and his Merry Men, I also left the outlaw a present – his one true love, Maid Marian.

TRUE   FALSE

Know Your Robot

I've encountered all sorts of mechanical menaces on my travels through space and time.

It pays to know your way around a sonic screwdriver when confronted by one of these robotic creatures, or even to have a mechanical pal of your own to help you out.

How many of these robot shadows do you recognise?

Famous Faces

When you get around the history of Earth as much as I do, sooner or later you're going to bump into some very famous faces indeed.

Can you work out which well-known names are hidden in the following anagrams?

1 **NEQUE TIFERITEN**
She joined me and various others aboard a Silurian Ark in the 24th century.

_ _ _ _ _ _   _ _ _ _ _ _ _ _ _ _

2 **MALIWIL REAPKAESHES**
He had a way with words that helped return the Carrionites to their eternal prison.

_ _ _ _ _ _ _   _ _ _ _ _ _ _ _ _ _

3 **DEAMMA ED DOOMPARPU**
She had a problem with things hiding under her bed, an unreliable clock and an even more unreliable fireplace.

_ _ _ _ _ _ _   _ _   _ _ _ _ _ _ _

4 **LARSHEC KIDSCEN**
Already famous for his festive ghosts, he ran into the gaseous Gelth in 19th-century Cardiff.

_ _ _ _ _ _ _   _ _ _ _ _ _ _

5 **UNEEQ CATRIVIO**
She once dubbed me Sir Doctor of TARDIS, before founding the Torchwood Institute.

_ _ _ _ _ _ _ _ _ _ _ _ _

6 **NINECTV AVN HOGG**
He had a thing for painting, sunflowers and Amy.

_ _ _ _ _ _ _ _ _ _ _ _ _ _

7 **HATGAA THIRSEIC**
This lady of letters helped me to defeat an insane Vespiform during a dinner party in the 1920s.

_ _ _ _ _ _ _ _ _ _ _ _ _ _

8 **FOLDA EITHRL**
I briefly bumped into this historical dictator after Mels suggested a trip to the Third Reich.

_ _ _ _ _ _ _ _ _ _ _

9 **NOTSWIN LURCHCHIL**
This wartime leader believed the Daleks were an invention of Dr Edwin Bracewell.

_ _ _ _ _ _ _ _ _ _ _ _ _ _ _ _

10 **BRINO DOHO**
I'm still not convinced that he was entirely real, but Clara certainly fell for his forest-y charm.

_ _ _ _ _ _ _ _ _

Man's Best Friend

They say that a man's best friend is his dog. If that's the case, then a Time Lord's best friend – aside from his current companion – must be his tin dog. And they don't come any more canny than K-9.

Could you ever make as vital a contribution as he did? Let's find out how much you know about my faithful friend. Simply match the questions below to the correct answer on the next page.

1 Who was K-9's inventor?

2 How many versions of K-9 have there been?

3 Which of my companions did the last version of K-9 remain with on Earth?

4 In which year was the original K-9 built?

5 What did K-9 wear round his neck?

6 The first time I met K-9, which alien menace did he help me to defeat?

Alien Attack!

Your planet Earth always seems to be under attack from one alien species or another. And now it's under attack again!

Write down the initial letters of the names of each alien species shown below to work out which one is after your homeworld this time.

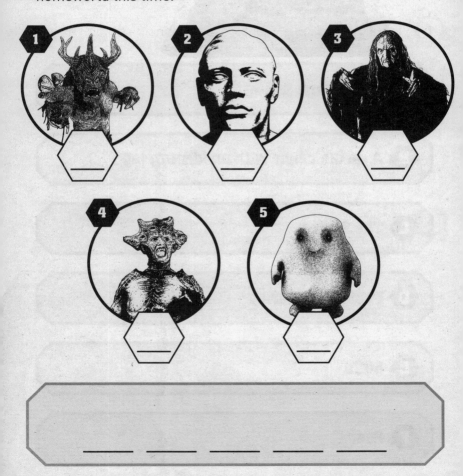

3D or Not 3D

Not all alien threats faced by the planet you call home come from beings that exist in the same set of dimensions as you.

Which of these alien incursions were in three dimensions and which weren't? In other words, 3D or not 3D? That is the question!

1 The angry Scribble Creature lurking inside Chloe Webber's wardrobe.

2 The black cubes that appeared on Earth during the year of the slow invasion.

3 The Boneless who created murals of missing people in Bristol.

4 The Zygons hiding in the Gallifreyan paintings kept in the Under Gallery of the National Gallery.

5 The personalities uploaded to the Nethersphere at the moment of their deaths.

Airlock Logic

Stranded at the end of the universe, Orson Pink's time capsule had an airlock on which he had written the words DON'T OPEN THE DOOR. But I unlocked it anyway.

Can you unlock the solution to this problem? Changing only one letter at each step, transform the word at the top of the word ladder into the one at the bottom. Can you make your way from **LOCK to OPEN?**

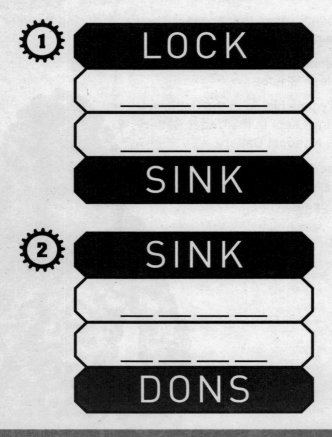

1

LOCK

_ _ _ _

_ _ _ _

SINK

2

SINK

_ _ _ _

_ _ _ _

DONS

3

DONS

_ _ _ _ _

_ _ _ _ _

EYES

4

EYES

_ _ _ _ _

_ _ _ _ _

_ _ _ _ _

OPEN

Time Lord Trials

Those who cannot remember the past are condemned to repeat it. That's what they say, isn't it? Well, it's as true of the Time Lords as it is of anybody else.

The Time Lords might once have been a noble race and a highly advanced civilisation, but they went through enough trials of their own. And now it's time for another trial for you. Can you work out the answers to these Time Lord-related riddles?

Home

In the star group of Kasterborous,

There once was a world most glorious.

With two moons and orange skies, they say,

This was the planet called _____ .

The Ultimate Enemy

These tentacled mutants from Skaro,

Over all worlds cast their dark shadow.

I met one once, covered in rusty flecks,

But you know them best as the _____ .

Behind Every Great Man

With the world on the brink of disaster,

Too often the cause was the Master.

You could never call him a sissy,

And now he's a she called _____ .

A Sort of Physician

This time-travelling TARDIS resident,

Was once of all Time Lords the president.

Poor Clara – too often he mocked her,

And you know him best as _____ _____ .

Do You Speak Gallifreyan?

Gallifrey was the home of the Time Lords. However at the conclusion of the Last Great Time War it was frozen in time and shunted into another dimension, by yours truly.

The language of Gallifrey is unlike anything you've ever seen. Can you crack this code and work out what the message says? (Of course, it's a highly simplified version of Gallifreyan, so even humans should be able to work it out.)

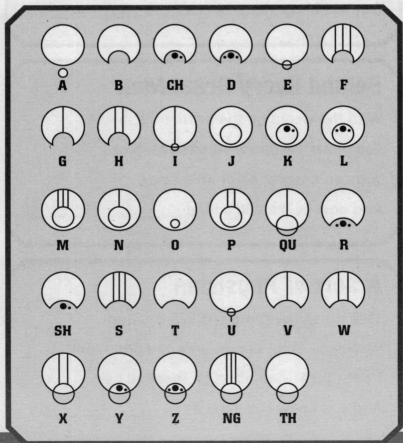

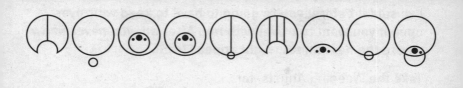

_____

_____   _____

_____

Don't Blink!

I've said it before: you're going to have to keep your eyes open if you want to travel with me. After all, you never know where the next threat might appear from.

Take the Weeping Angels, for example. If you don't keep a close eye on them you're done for. Quantum-locked until you look away and then *BANG*! You're living out your days back in the past.

Scan these two pictures and work out what's missing or changed between them. But remember: don't blink!

DECENT DOCTOR

So you still think you've got what it takes to travel with a Time Lord, do you?

Well you've made it this far and you haven't turned back yet, I'll give you that. You clearly don't need me holding your hand any more.

If you were a Time Lord I'd say it's like you've worn in your new body and got over the tricky post-regeneration phase – but you're not, so I won't.

You're still going to need your wits about you – such as they are – as you embark on the next part of your test to prove your worth to me.

What's that? Bring it on, you say? OK then. I will!

Biological Brain-teasers

We Time Lords might look human – although, really, since we're the older race I should say you humans look Time Lord – but beneath our familiar and handsome exteriors we are most definitely *not* human.

See if you can answer these questions about Gallifreyan physiology. They're fairly tricky, but I've given multiple-choice answers to help you out.

1 How many hearts does a Time Lord have?

TWO	THREE

2 So how many pulses are there to a Time Lord heartbeat?

FOUR	SIX

3 How many times can a Time Lord regenerate in a standard regenerative cycle?

TWELVE	THIRTEEN

4 How many times faster than a human's are a Time Lord's reactions?

TEN

TWENTY

5 For how many minutes can a Time Lord survive the sub-zero temperatures of space?

SIX

SIXTEEN

6 How old was I when I looked into the Untempered Schism on Gallifrey?

EIGHT

EIGHTEEN

7 How many billion languages can I speak?

FIVE

FIFTY

8 How many of my incarnations encountered and defeated the rogue Time Lord Omega in the anti-matter universe?

THREE

FIVE

BONUS POINT: If you add all the correct answers together, you'll get the number of years that passed on Earth between my first companion attending Coal Hill School and Clara starting to teach there.

The Sonic

My pal Clara once asked me if I could explain a plan to her without using the words 'sonic screwdriver'. Well, how about using the words 'sonic cane' or 'sonic sunglasses'?

My companions, and sometimes my enemies, have made use of all sorts of sonic devices. Question is, can you fit all of them into this sonic-themed word grid?

Eight letters

SONIC GUN
SONIC PEN

Nine letters

SONIC CANE
SONIC CONE

Ten letters

SONIC KNIFE
SONIC LANCE
SONIC PROBE

Twelve letters

SONIC BLASTER

Thirteen letters

SONIC LIPSTICK

Fifteen letters

SONIC DOOR HANDLE

Sixteen letters

SONIC SCREWDRIVER
ULTRASONIC RAY GUN

Don't Tell

Once, I found myself lost inside the Bank of Karabraxos, the most secure financial institution in the galaxy. No one could step foot on Karabraxos without protocols, all movement was monitored, air consumption was regulated and DNA checks were required at every stage.

As if that wasn't bad enough, Ms Delphox, the Head of Bank Security, had employed the Teller – an alien being that scanned the minds of all who visited the bank for criminal intent. If it detected guilt, it would liquefy the guilty party's brain.

The question is: with the puny brain power you have at your disposal, can you find your way through the labyrinthine corridors to the heart of the Bank of Karabraxos, whilst also avoiding the Teller?

START

FINISH

Journey to the Centre of the TARDIS

The TARDIS has been described in many ways: as a remarkable accomplishment of transdimensional engineering, bigger on the inside and as an impossible blue box.

I once journeyed to the centre of the TARDIS with my good friend Clara. Can you achieve the same feat by answering each of these questions in turn and filling in the spiralling word grid?

1 The TARDIS is bigger on the inside because it is . . . (13,14)

2 What is it that gives a Time Lord a biological link to his TARDIS? (8,10)

3 What does the TARDIS contain that is disguised as an art gallery? (9,5,7)

4 The logo of which organisation appears on the door of the TARDIS? (2,4,9)

5 Where on the TARDIS can you find an ivy-covered colonnade and the sound of birdsong? (8,4)

6 The TARDIS is powered by the Eye of Harmony, an exploding star in the process of becoming a black hole, suspended in a permanent . . . (5,2,5)

7 One of the other elements the TARDIS needs to function is found in Time Lord brains, and the bodies of other time travellers. What is it? (6,6)

8 The TARDIS usually travels through time and space through the . . . (4,6)

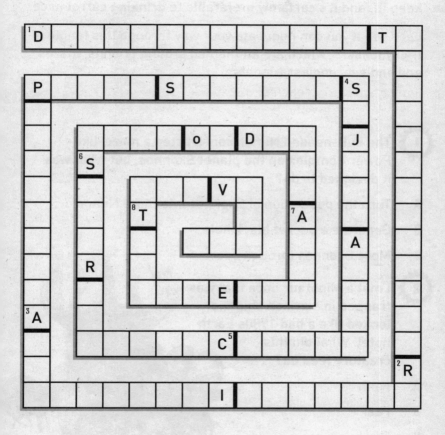

An Awful Lot of Running

My companions and I always seem to find ourselves running down endless corridors in our efforts to escape whatever maze we've found ourselves in. I suppose it's a good way to keep fit, and it's certainly preferable to drinking carrot juice.

Let's see if you can negotiate your way through this tangle of tricky teasers, which are all themed around prisons, mazes, and endless, endless tunnels.

1 The bull-headed Nimon constructed a maze-like Power Complex on the planet Skonnos, but what was it designed to do?

A   Turn the population of Skonnos into more Nimon

B   Generate a pocket black hole

C   Move Skonnos through space

2 I met a Minotaur once that was trapped in a prison ship that looked like a bad 1980s Earth hotel. What did this creature feed on?

A   Faith

B   Fear

C   Flesh

3 Castrovalva was a city created using Block Transfer Computation and Adric's mathematical genius – but it deliberately folded in on itself, trapping my companions and me. Who had set the trap?

A Omega

B The Valeyard

C The Master

4 The Pandorica was a prison designed by the Alliance to contain me. Where was it hidden?

A On Skaro

B In the British Museum

C Beneath Stonehenge

5 Robin Hood, Clara and I were once captured by the Sheriff of Nottingham and imprisoned in the dungeons of Nottingham Castle, but how did Hood and I escape?

A Using the guard's keys

B Using my sonic screwdriver

C By uprooting the posts we had been chained to

6 In the 21st century, which group used the Tower of London as its headquarters?

A Torchwood

B UNIT

C The Winders

7 What was the name of the prison where River Song spent her days, having supposedly killed me at Lake Silencio?

A Stormcage

B The Vault

C Demons Run

8 At the end of the Last Great Time War I trapped Gallifrey in a pocket universe, but how many incarnations of me were needed to achieve this?

A Three

B Eleven

C Thirteen

9 When House possessed my TARDIS, Amy and Rory were forced to flee deeper and deeper inside it, but where did they eventually take refuge?

A In the library

B In the archived coral console room

C In the Eye of Harmony

10 On Alfava Metraxis,
Amy and I joined Father
Octavian and his men in
a network of catacombs
called the Maze of the
Dead, but which alien
foe was he hunting?

A Weeping Angels

B The Silence

C Cybermen

11 Clara once confessed to me that she hated catacombs;
where were we at the time?

A In the Underhenge

B Beneath the battlefield graveyard on Trenzalore

C Lost inside the TARDIS

12 The TARDIS created several space loops using the
corridors to keep Tricky Van Baalen and me trapped
in a labyrinth because Gregor Van Baalen had stolen
which item?

A A piece of the TARDIS's architectural
reconfiguration system

B A magno-grab remote

C Part of the time rotor

TARDIS Transformations

I change my TARDIS desktop about as often as I change my face – more often, in fact. But do you know which face went with which console-room makeover?

Here's a clue to help you: I had a thing for the coral setting during my grunge period.

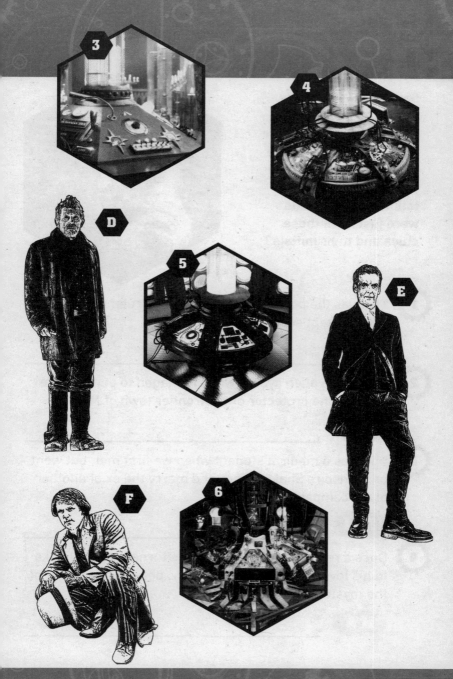

Memory Worm Mysteries

Say you inadvertently picked up a Memory Worm instead of a sonic screwdriver or a phone (it's easily done). Could you work out who the following individuals were just from these clues and their initials?

1 She was the porcelain-mask-wearing ruler of *Starship UK* who kept secrets from herself.

L T _____

2 He was an alien cyborg who I managed to persuade to become the protector of the frontier town of Mercy.

K T _____

3 She was a medical student when we first met, but went on to inspire Shakespeare and marry the ex of another of my companions.

M J _____

4 Once a respected naval officer, he turned rogue thanks to his love of gold. His ship, *Fancy*, became the target of the mysterious Siren.

H A _____

5 A generation 5000 soldier, she was a child of the Progenation Machine and, at the same time, my daughter. Sort of.

J _____

6 My landlord (for a while) and my friend, husband to Sophie and father to Stormageddon.

C O _____

7 I knew her father, once upon a time, when he ran UNIT, which is now her job.

K S _____

8 He thought he was me for a while, although his faithful companion was called Rosita and his TARDIS was actually a hot-air balloon.

J L _____

9 Defender of humanity and, as a result, the loneliest man in the universe. I caught up with him on Hedgewick's World, where we battled against the Cybermen.

P _____

10 A keen amateur astronomer, wise and gentle. He was also the man who knocked four times, forcing my irradiated body to regenerate once again.

W M _____

Alien A to Z

From the Abzorbaloff to the Zygons, I've met them all. But can you identify the following twenty-six alien races with the help of the clues? Simply circle the correct answer in each case.

A is for . . .

These aliens were made of living fat.

| Androgum | Adipose | Axons |

B is for . . .

A race of 2D beings from another reality.

| Blowfish | Bannermen | Boneless |

C is for . . .

The advanced science of these aliens appeared much like magic and voodoo to more primitive minds.

| Carrionites | Catkind | Chimeron |

D is for . . .

An evil race of genetically engineered aliens from the planet Skaro. I thought I met a good one once. Turned out it was just malfunctioning.

| Draconians | Dæmons | Daleks |

E is for . . .

Parasitic aliens that inhabit human bodies and have a green eye-stalk that can look out of their host's mouth.

| Eternals | Exxilons | Eknodines |

F is for . . .

Large, eyeless and limbless creatures with a fringe of pink tentacles round their mouths from the original fifth planet of the solar system.

| Fendahleen | The Flood | Foamasi |

G is for . . .

Gaseous life forms that lost their bodies as a result of the Time War.

| Gangers | Gelth | Gastropods |

H is for . . .

Amphibious fish-headed humanoid soldiers.

Haemovores	Hoix	Hath

I is for . . .

Reptilian Martians. Big, scaly and scary.

Ice Warriors	Isolus	Inter Minorians

J is for . . .

A race of rhinocerous-esque humanoids. Good at doing as they're told.

Judoon	Jagrafess	Jagaroth

K is for . . .

Space-travelling griffin-like predators that are invisible to most people.

Kastrians	Krafayis	Krynoids

L is for . . .

A race of humanoid mathematicians known for their ability to do Block Transfer Computations in their heads, without the aid of even a blackboard.

Logopolitans	Lakertyans	Lady Cassandra

M is for . . .

Gigantic crustaceans that fed on gas.

Malmooth	Mandrels	Macra

N is for . . .

Minotaur-like creatures known to impersonate gods.

Nestene	Nimon	Nostrovites

O is for . . .

Silicon-based life forms with a thirst for blood.

Ogri	Ogrons	Osirans

P is for . . .

Stone-skinned creatures made of living magma.

| Plasmavores | Pyroviles | Peladonians |

R is for . . .

These flatulent aliens are grouped into extended families, hatch from eggs and have an aversion to vinegar.

| Racnoss | Rutans | Raxacoricofallapatorians |

S is for . . .

Vampiric fish-lobsters.

| Saturnynes | Sea Devils | Sycorax |

T is for . . .

Bat-like aliens with four ears, four eyes and a forked tongue that injects venom.

| Tharils | Terileptils | Tetraps |

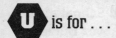 **is for** . . .

Lumpy-featured, green-skinned humanoids that secrete poison from glands on their necks which compresses organic matter.

| Urbankans | Uvodni | Usurians |

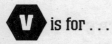 **is for** . . .

Carnivorous, flesh-devouring shadows.

| Vespiform | Vinvocci | Vashta Nerada |

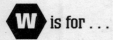 **is for** . . .

Faceless beings that worked for the Great Intelligence. Always spoke in rhyme, which got very irritating very quickly.

| Whisper Men | Wirrn | Weeping Angels |

   is for . . .

Shape-shifting bodysnatchers from a long-dead planet, and masters of the Skarasen.

| Xeraphin | Yeti | Zygons |

Take Care

On one occasion I went undercover at Coal Hill School as the new caretaker. My plan was to trap a rogue Skovox Blitzer there by placing chronodyne generators around the school.

Look at the plan of Coal Hill School below and place one of six types of chronodyne generator (numbered 1 to 6) in each room, so that no number appears more than once in any row or column of the grid.

SCHOOL HALL — CARETAKER'S WORKSHOP

		2		5	3		4
			6			2	

ENGLISH CLASSROOM / MATHS CLASSROOM

1			5		2
5		4			1
	5			1	
6		1	2		3

STAFFROOM — DINING HALL

School's Out!

They say your school days are the best of your life – well, so long as a race of planet-grabbing aliens doesn't attempt to take over your school as part of their nefarious plan, that is.

The aliens in question often hide in plain sight, usually as members of staff. Can you find the alien races hiding in plain sight in these anagrams?

1 SITKAENILRL

_ _ _ _ _ _ _ _ _ _ _

2 HET YIFLMA FO DLOBO

_ _ _ _ _ _ _ _ _ _ _ _ _ _ _

3 SKALDE

_ _ _ _ _ _

4 ELTHESIN

_ _ _ _ _ _ _ _

5 VOOKXS ZITRELB

_ _ _ _ _ _ _ _ _ _ _ _

Coal Hill Conundrums

My connection to Coal Hill School goes way back, but it's not just me. A number of my companions have connections to the school too. I don't know what it is about the place, but it's also had its unfair share of attention from hostile alien forces.

Can you choose the correct answers to the following questions about Coal Hill School, or has your own education been sadly lacking?

1 Where is Coal Hill School?

> **East London**   **West London**

2 How was I related to pupil Susan Foreman?

> **Grandfather**   **Uncle**

3 What subject did Barbara Wright teach, causing her to clash with Susan?

> **History**   **Maths**

4 Barbara travelled with me through time and space, along with Coal Hill's science teacher. What was his name?

> **Ian**   **Steven**

5 In later years, that science teacher was promoted to what position at the school?

> **Headmaster**   **Dean**

6 In 1963 Coal Hill was invaded by a renegade group of Daleks. What were they trying to locate?

Hand of Omega

Foot of Omega

7 What did my companion Ace use to take out one of the Daleks in the school science lab?

Baseball bat

Cricket bat

8 Which Coal Hill pupil would one day become President of the United States?

Courtney Woods

Courtney Leaves

9 Danny Pink led training sessions with which group at the school?

Cadet Squad

Maths Squad

10 Why did I decide that the school was a suitable location to lure the Skovox Blitzer to?

It's quiet at night

It has a big hall

In the Pink

Danny Pink, aka PE, grew very close to Clara while they were working together at Coal Hill School, even though he wasn't my biggest fan. But how much do you know about Dan the soldier man?

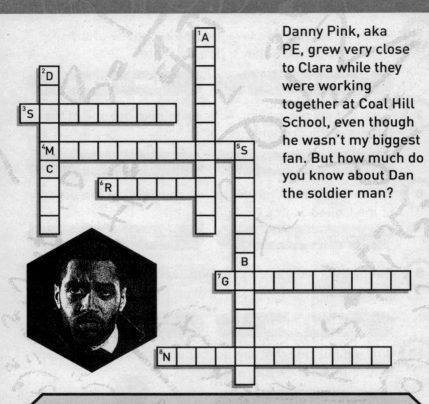

ACROSS

3 What was Danny's rank when he served in the British Army? (8)

4 What subject did Danny teach at Coal Hill School? (11)

6 What was Danny's real name? (6)

7 Where was the children's home in which Danny grew up? (10)

8 Danny found himself here after he was knocked down by a car. (12)

DOWN

1 Danny did a tour of duty in this Asian country when he was in the army. (11)

2 Clara saw Danny dressed as Santa Claus when under the influence of this alien parasite. (5,4)

5 Danny disabled a number of chronodyne generators which I was using to capture this rogue war robot. (6,7)

Noble Sacrifice

River Song made the ultimate sacrifice so that others might live, but she hasn't been the only one to do so.

Can you find the names of my companions and other acquaintances who risked everything to protect the futures of millions in these anagrams?

1 NYNAD KIPN

_ _ _ _ _ _ _ _ _

2 CIDAR

_ _ _ _ _

3 ITSRAD THEP

_ _ _ _ _ _ _ _ _

4 YAM NODP

_ _ _ _ _ _ _

5 KIMYEC MITHS

_ _ _ _ _ _ _ _ _ _

6 ONDAN LENBO

_ _ _ _ _ _ _ _ _ _

What's in the Wi-Fi?

I remember when something was hiding in the Wi-Fi. Something sinister. Something that fed on people's minds. Something I had met and defeated many times before.

That's right – it was the Great Intelligence, up to its old tricks. My genius proved to be superior once again, but how would you have fared? Work out how to transform one word into another on the four word ladders, changing only one letter at a time.

1 When Clara called me wanting help with her Wi-Fi, I was living as a monk. Can you get from MONK to HELP in eight steps?

MONK

_ _ _ _

_ _ _ _

_ _ _ _

BULK

_ _ _ _

_ _ _ _

HELP

2 Miss Kizlet used her hi-tech tablet to hack people's personalities. Can you get from TABLET to HACKED in eight steps?

TABLET

— — — — — —

— — — — — —

— — — — — —

CALLED

— — — — — —

— — — — — —

— — — — — —

HACKED

SPOON

— — — — — —

— — — — — —

— — — — — —

STORE
STARE

— — — — — —

— — — — — —

— — — — — —

— — — — — —

HEADS

3 The Spoonheads were robotic servers created to help the Great Intelligence upload people's minds to the Cloud. Can you get from SPOON to HEADS in nine steps?

Kill the Moon

There was one time when Clara and I ended up on the moon only to find it falling apart around us – as our friendship did too for a while afterwards. Turned out the moon was really an egg, which hatched and released a space-dragon thing. Don't you just hate it when that happens?

Can you work out which piece of the moon's broken shell is required to complete the puzzle on the opposite page? Circle the piece when you find it!

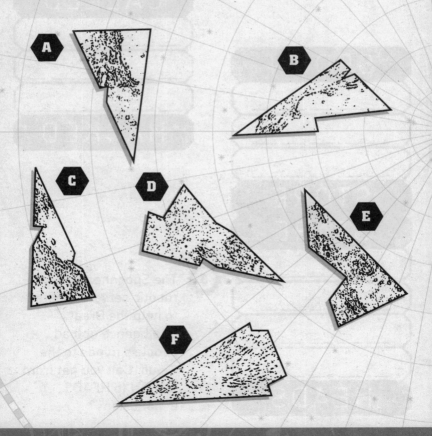

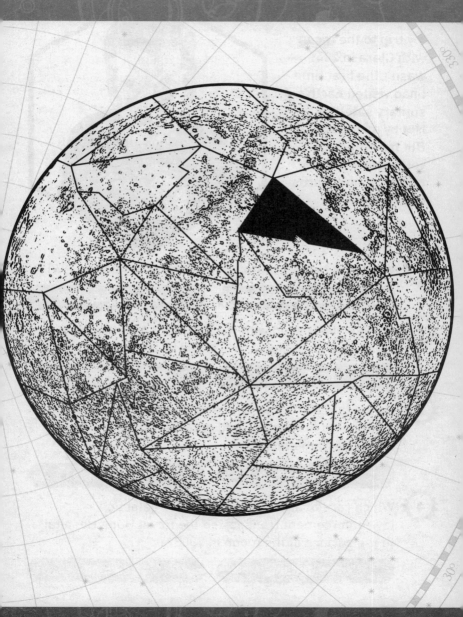

Moon Mysteries

My trip to the moon with Clara in 2049 wasn't the first time I had visited Earth's solitary satellite. Not by a long shot. But how much do you know about my previous adventures on the moon?

1 What was hidden on the dark side of the moon in 1941?

A Dalek flying saucer   **A giant Cyberman**

2 In 1969 I interfered with the *Apollo 11* moon landing transmission to stop which group of aliens?

The Silence   **The Zygons**

3 By the late 20th century, which race of cybernetically augmented humanoids had established a base on the dark side of the moon?

The Cybermen   **The Silurians**

4 Which race of aliens responsible for galactic law-enforcement transported the Royal Hope Hospital to the surface of the moon in 2008?

The Judoon   **The Flood**

5 By 2049 there were giant red-and-black spider-like creatures living in caves on the moon, but what were they really?

Germs

Robots

6 Who graduated from Luna University with a degree in archaeology in the year 5123?

River Song

Clara Oswald

7 How many moons did the Earth have in the time of the Fourth Great and Bountiful Human Empire?

Five

Twenty

8 I once concentrated moonlight into a laser-like beam in order to save Queen Victoria from the Host, but which stately Scottish home were we in at the time?

Torchwood House

UNIT Manor

9 An artificial moon maintained the computer systems of the library via a wireless connection, but what was it called?

Doctor Moon

Lord Lunar

10 Where did I find the lost moon of Poosh? (Clue: it wasn't hidden down the back of the sofa.)

In the Medusa Cascade

Next to Adipose 3

Lost Worlds

When the New Dalek Empire tried to bring about the end of reality itself, they used an engine made up of twenty-seven heavenly bodies which they had stolen from throughout space and time.

Can you find the names of nine of those lost worlds hidden within this wordsearch?

```
T Z L X K D A D B R H L O Q T
A G S H F P S P R O X U O Q Z
D D X Q T C O A P N S P H G T
C L O M R O P X F I K P A T I
E X Z K U R F G K M A T J X S
V S Y T F Z H F U X L P O R H
E R S X U G Y P I A Y Q Z J A
A D I P O S E T H R E E W R L
S B R Z Y V V C O F G D F G L
K Q N E H H K V L U X V T R A
R L H T X T I J H L Y X K B C
H Y R B W L U U W L X O H A A
K A F A L D L H P A I L Z S T
E N H I C H E S H C U V O K O
W O A S G T P E W N A M O W P
```

PYROVILLIA

ADIPOSE THREE

CALLUFRAX MINOR

JAHOO

SHALLACATOP

WOMAN WEPT

CLOM

GRIFFOTH

EARTH

Cascade Coordinates

The Daleks transported the stolen planets to the Medusa Cascad, which is located at the centre of a rift in time and space. Using the star map coordinates given below, can you plot the positions of the remaining nine planets (plus the Lost Moon of Poosh) inside the Medusa Cascade?

Adipose 3 (4,4)   Griffoth (7,9)   Pyrovillia (10,4)
Callufrax Minor (3,8) Jahoo (7,1)   Shallacatop (13,9)
Clom (2,12)   Lost Moon of Poosh   Woman Wept (12,2)
Earth (7,7)   (8,11)

Arachnophobia

Tell me, what are you afraid of? The dark? Eerie silences? That ticking you can hear coming from under the bed?

What about spiders? How about giant spiders with psychic powers? Or the four-billion-year-old queen of all spiders, armed with a laser-gun-toting starship?

Well, I've met them all. All you have to do is find the nine spider-related words listed below in the web of letters on the opposite page.

METEBELIS III

EIGHT LEGS

RACNOSS

WEBSTAR

EMPRESS

SECRET HEART

ACTEON GALAXY

MOON

SPIDER GERMS

```
Z I N V Z Y N T U M J X X D R
A C T E O N G A L A X Y B G A
T N J A O X S P I X A K U M C
F I U O S F H L U T U T F E N
C H M G Z K R A T S B E W T O
N T R A E H T E R C E S Y E S
Q U T G X I C D T Z R L D B S
E I G H T L E G S G M G U E F
D S P I D E R G E R M S S L Y
B J G V D H C P C B Y I Q I J
B P B G M J N J C O Y R X S B
R O B V U Z R P S M Q H I Q
K F W X F P I B K M M H R I J
D A R K N G T Y C C V M G I M
X N H Z E C Q E M P R E S S H
```

In Case of Emergency

Who do you call when the planet's in peril? Who else but me? The Doctor – the man who stops the monsters! But where can my companions and I turn in times of trouble? That's right – to the TARDIS!

The TARDIS comes equipped with all manner of defensive mechanisms and clever features, but do you know your HADS from your DITO?

 1 **What does HADS stand for?**

A   Hostile Action Displacement System

B   Hostile Action Defence System

C   Happy Action Displacement System

2 What is the name of the TARDIS's internal alarm system which rings when the vessel is in danger?

A The Emergency Bell

B The Cloister Bell

C The Danger Bell

3 What is the name of the device that returns the TARDIS to a previous location in space and time?

A The Fast Return Switch

B The Time Switch Lever

C The Flip Back Switch

4 The TARDIS has a secondary control room, just in case the primary control room should be temporarily out of action. True or false?

TRUE   **FALSE**

5 What is the name of the device that rewrites the biology of one species so that its cells appear to be those of another?

A The Chameleon Portal

B The Chameleon Chair

C The Chameleon Arch

6 I once created perception filters for myself, Martha Jones and Captain Jack Harkness, which activated when they were worn round the neck. What did I make them from?

A TARDIS keys

B Coat buttons

C Bow ties

7 If the TARDIS materialises in a space occupied by another object, that object can appear inside the TARDIS. True or false?

TRUE **FALSE**

8 I once passed a magno-grab remote through a crack in time to my younger self in order to to save my time machine. Which three words did I inscribe on the remote's side?

A Big Fun Button

B Big Fearsome Button

C Big Friendly Button

9 If the time machine's shields fail, what is its last line of defence, activated using a lever located under the TARDIS's console?

A Siege Mode

B Invisibility Mode

C Bulletproof Mode

10 If it needs more power to take off, the TARDIS can discard some of its own rooms! True or false?

TRUE **FALSE**

11 Finally, what is the purpose of Emergency Program One?

A It summons a Time Lord official to the TARDIS

B It returns a companion to a safe place away from any danger

C It gives the Eye of Harmony an extra boost of energy

The Sands of Time

The sands of time. Time out. All in good time. Time flies. Right on time. Borrowed time . . . I've heard them all. Silly human expressions about the passage of timey-wimey stuff.

One time, I ran into a mummy in space, on board the Orient Express. I definitely thought Clara and I were out of time on that occasion.

Anyway, you now have all the time in the world to solve this puzzle. All you have to do is work out how much time the clocks are changing by and then add the correct time to the final clock face in each sequence.

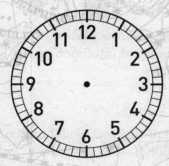

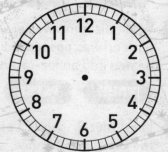

The clocks are going forward by _____ minutes.

How Great Is Your Intelligence?

Clearly not that great, since you're only a human being and not a Time Lord – but maybe you remember a thing or two from my various encounters with the Great Intelligence.

For example, do you know where the so-called Great Intelligence originated from? No?

OK, let's make it a little easier for you. Simply answer true or false to the following statements.

1 Doctor Simeon established the GI Institute in the 19th century.

TRUE   FALSE

2 When his mind was erased by a Memory Worm, Doctor Simeon was possessed by the Great Intelligence and turned into an ice-faced vampire.

TRUE   FALSE

3 I first met Brigadier Lethbridge-Stewart whilst battling the Great Intelligence, although he was still only a colonel then.

TRUE   FALSE

4 In 2013, the Great Intelligence was back, invading everyone's homes through their TVs.

TRUE   FALSE

5 The Great Intelligence was working for Miss Kizlet.

TRUE   FALSE

6 Miss Kizlet had a tablet computer that could hack human minds.

TRUE   FALSE

7 The Great Intelligence once tried to take over London's sewers with its yetis.

TRUE   FALSE

8 The yetis were actually fur-covered robots controlled by the Great Intelligence.

TRUE   FALSE

9 The Whisper Men were also servants of the Great Intelligence.

TRUE   FALSE

10 Jenny Flint once described the Great Intelligence as 'a body without a mind'.

TRUE   FALSE

They say that behind every great Time Lord there's a great companion. I've had plenty of great companions in my life, but how much do you know about them? See if you can name the companions from my clues.

1 She was my first travelling companion after I fled Gallifrey, having stolen the TARDIS.

_____

2 A trained journalist, her nose for a good story often got her into trouble. Good pals with K-9.

_____

3 A warrior of the Sevateem tribe and quite savage when I first met her. I did my best to educate and civilise her, curbing her more violent tendencies.

_____

4 This chatty Australian air hostess described herself as 'a mouth on legs'.

_____

5 She helped me to defeat the Master on New Year's Eve 1999 after accidentally killing me on the operating table.

_____

6 She was an ordinary shop girl when we first met and defeated the Nestene Consciousness together, but by the time we parted she was anything but ordinary.

_____

7 Plagued by the ticking that came from under her bed, this young lady made such an impression that they named a starship after her in the 51st century.

_____

8 She became a waitress on board the cruise liner spaceship *Titanic* with the romantic notion of seeing the universe.

---

9 I proposed to this one-time Queen of England, believing her to be a Zygon in disguise. (It's a long story.) When we next met in 1599, at the Globe Theatre, she ordered her guards to cut off my head!

---

10 After the Weeping Angels trapped Martha Jones and me in 1969 without the TARDIS, we needed this clever and courageous photographer to rescue us. Trouble was, the only way we could communicate was through Easter Eggs hidden in her DVD collection.

---

11 I once accidentally accepted a marriage proposal from this Hollywood star, making her my third wife – but Norma Jean Mortensen was better known by her screen name.

---

12 This rich aristocrat got her kicks from stealing precious artefacts, such as the priceless Cup of Athelstan. Her escape from the scene of the crime aboard a London bus took her to the planet of San Helios.

_____

13 Once upon a time, a history teacher called John Smith fell in love with the kindly matron at Farringham School for Boys. She had no idea that John Smith was really me in disguise, until the Family of Blood hunted me down and tried to kill her. Poor woman.

_____

14 What can I say about this enigmatic and flirtatious time-travelling archaeology professor? Whatever clues I might give you would all be spoilers.

_____

15 A riddle, wrapped in a mystery, inside an enigma – for a long time I called her the Impossible Girl. Who knows where our adventures might take us next? Wherever we end up, I'm sure it will be magical.

_____

Child of the TARDIS

Ah, River Song. If I bothered with things like the internet, I would have to list our relationship status as 'complicated', mainly because we kept meeting in the wrong order.

It took me a while to discover who she really was, but how about you? How much do you know about this child of the TARDIS? Try completing these sentences and let's find out.

1 River Song's birthplace was the

_____ asteroid.

2 When River was at school (with her parents), she went

by the nickname _____ .

3 She was conditioned by Madame Kovarian and the

Silence to kill _____ .

4 River Song's real name is _____ .

5 River was able to travel through time using a

_____ .

6 She kept track of her adventures with me in a diary that

looked a lot like the _____ .

7 River gave her life for the 4,000 people saved in the

computer system of the _____ .

'Hello, Sweetie'

It was a – what do you call it? – a catchphrase of hers, just like how I used to enjoy saying 'Fantastic!' or 'Allons-y!' or 'Geronimo!'

But can you match the first thing River Song said to me to the occasion when we ran into each other?

1. Hello, Sweetie.

3. All right, then. Where are we? Have we done Easter Island yet?

A. Lake Silencio in Utah, 23 April 2011.

B. When the Weeping Angels tried to take over Manhattan in the 1930s.

2. And what sort of time do you call this?

C. At the National Museum in 1996, when the exploding TARDIS had brought about the end of the universe.

D. After the Battle of Demons Run.

E. When the Vashta Nerada invaded the Library.

4. Well, soldier, how goes the day?

5. When one's in love with an ageless god who insists on the face of a twelve-year-old, one does one's best to hide the damage.

Timey-wimey Crossword

As I once said, time is like a big ball of wibbly-wobbly, timey-wimey stuff. (It wasn't my finest hour.) Whether it's an abstract concept or a tangible fourth dimension, there's no escaping it, and you human beings have always been obsessed with measuring it.

But apparently something as simple as a fob watch can be invaluable to a Time Lord too. Can you work out the answers to the following clock-related crossword clues and fit them into the grid on the opposite page?

ACROSS

3 My eighth incarnation stole the beryllium chip from one of these on the eve of the Millennium. (6,5)

6 Captain Jack tethered his ship here in January 1941, but this famous clock tower was later destroyed by a Slitheen craft crashing into it. (3,3)

7 The Master's TARDIS appeared to be one of these big old clocks on the planet Traken, thanks to its functioning chameleon circuit. (11,5)

8 I made my last stand against the Daleks in this building in the town of Christmas on the planet Trenzalore. (5,5)

DOWN

1 My second incarnation had one of these time-telling devices on board the TARDIS, even though there was no natural sunlight inside the time machine. (7)

2 These robots broke clocks to hide the ticking of their own internal workings. (9,6)

4 This device granted the wearer the ability to vanish from view. (12,5)

5 It is said that the essence of a Time Lord can be contained within one of these. (3,5)

TRUE TIME LORD

So, how did you get on with that last lot of questions? Found them tough, I bet. A little bit tricky, I suspect.

Well, wait until you see what's coming up next. Even the giant Ood Brain would struggle with some of these cerebral challenges, while the mathematicians of the planet Logopolis would take at least a week to calculate answers to the algebraic teasers I've invented for you.

Put it this way: if you can conquer these logic problems, you must be almost as clever as me.

Almost.

Spoilers!

The trouble with being a Time Lord is that major events in my own life don't always take place in the right order. It makes weddings and funerals particularly complicated.

I have encountered various people during my travels who have known things about my future, but which of the following spoilers are true and which are false?

1 I first met River Song in the Library, although she had clearly already met me.

TRUE FALSE

2 When the Moment took on a human form to persuade me not to activate it and thereby destroy Gallifrey, it took the form of my future companion Clara Oswald.

TRUE FALSE

3 On Trenzalore, when I was still in my eleventh incarnation, I visited the one place I should never go: my own tomb.

TRUE FALSE

4 In my seventh incarnation, I met the sorceress Morgaine. She recognised me – even though I had not met her before – and called me Merlin.

TRUE   FALSE

5 Sally Sparrow gave me a transcript of a conversation we hadn't had yet just as Donna Noble and I were trying to stop a migration involving four things and a lizard.

TRUE   FALSE

6 When I met Idris – my TARDIS, in human form – one of the first things she said to me was 'Goodbye' rather than 'Hello'.

TRUE   FALSE

7 In my first incarnation I contacted two of my future replacements, and asked them if I was having a midlife crisis.

TRUE   FALSE

8 My future self – aka the Architect – set me the challenge of breaking into the Bank of Karabraxos.

TRUE   FALSE

Flatlined

The Boneless were something I had never encountered, until I ran into them on the mean streets of Bristol. Two-dimensional beings from another universe, they were able to reduce 3D objects into 2D forms, which proved fatal for human beings and forced me to engage the TARDIS's siege mode.

Look at the 3D picture below of the TARDIS in siege mode, then work out which of the two-dimensional nets on the opposite page could be used to create it.

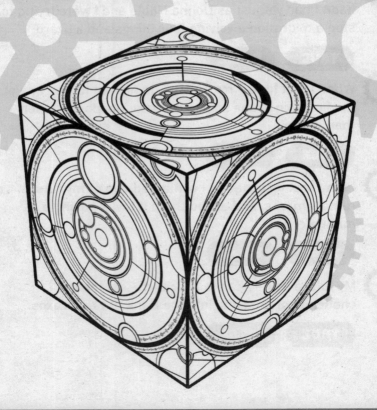

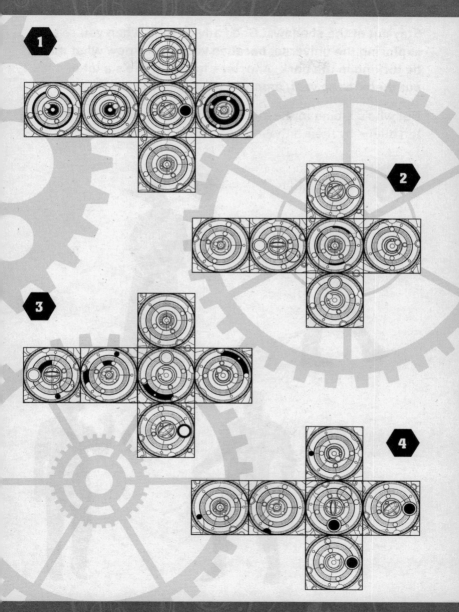

Hiding in the Shadows

Stay out of the shadows! Good advice that, when you're exploring the universe, because you never know what might be lurking in the dark. And, let's face it, there's a lot of dark out there in the vast, empty expanses of the void.

But who's hiding in the shadows here? Can you identify these ten aliens by their silhouettes alone?

The Bells

I suppose it's my own fault for travelling around the universe in a police telephone box, but I always seem to be on call. If it's not people ringing me up asking for help, it's the TARDIS's own cloister bell chiming and warning me of approaching danger.

If you're going to travel in time and space, you should know what to do in an emergency. So let's see if you can connect these questions with the appropriate answers.

1 Why did the cloister bell ring when the TARDIS crashed in Amy Pond's garden?

A   The TARDIS's engines were phasing

B   There was a crack in space and time in Amy's bedroom

C   Prisoner Zero was hiding in her house

2 When the cloister bell rang on the planet Shan Shen, which two words suddenly appeared everywhere, including on the exterior of the TARDIS itself?

A   Doctor Who?

B   Bad Wolf

C   Hello, Sweetie

3 The cloister bell also rang when the Master stole my TARDIS, but what had he done to cause it distress?

A   He had engaged siege mode

B   He had tried to travel beyond the end of the universe

C   He had turned it into a Paradox Machine

4 When Clara phoned the TARDIS thinking she was phoning a tech support line, who did she say had given her the number?

A Missy

B Miss Kizlet

C A woman in a shop

5 When Winston Churchill phoned me on the TARDIS phone, what was he face-to-face with?

A A Cyberman

B A Silurian

C A Dalek

6 When Earth was trapped in the Medusa Cascade, my friends sent me a signal by forcing every telephone on the planet to call the same number at the same time. Who was it that had my number saved on their phone?

A Martha Jones

B Rose Tyler

C Donna Noble

7 Whose call to the TARDIS phone ultimately sent me to rob the Bank of Karabraxos?

A The Architect

B Ms Delphox

C Ms Karabraxos

As if negotiating the corridors of the Bank of Karabraxos wasn't bad enough, when I eventually found my way to Ms Karabraxos's private vault, I had to crack the code to get inside. Could you do the same?

Match these shapes to the four letter grids below, substituting each symbol for the corresponding letter. The letters will spell out the secret password!

□ ⟩ ⌐⌐ ⟩   ∨ ⟩ ⌐· ⌐⌐ ⟩ □ ⊓ ⌐ ⌃

_____ _____

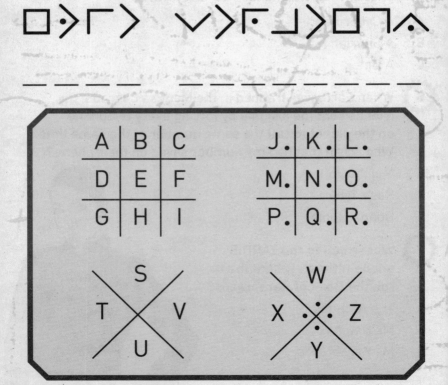

Trouble³

I've never really known why but trouble somehow always manages to find me, even when I don't go looking for it.

I'm like a trouble magnet. And sometimes that trouble is so bad, it's like trouble squared – or, if it's *really* bad, trouble cubed. Speaking of which, do you know what these cube-type things are? Clue: all of them have caused me trouble!

1

2

3

4

5

6

Time War History

The Last Great Time War isn't something I really like to talk about. For several hundred years I believed I'd wiped out the Time Lords, along with the Daleks, in order to end an eternity of conflict.

That said, it helped make me the man I am today. So how much do you know about the events of the most cataclysmic battle in all creation?

1 In the final stages of the Time War, how many flying saucers did the Daleks have?

_____ **million**

2 Over the course of the war, the Time Lords deployed every forbidden weapon in the Omega Arsenal. Where were these weapons kept?

The _____ _____ **on Gallifrey**

3 There was only one weapon that the Time Lords dared not use. What was it?

The M _____

4 During the Time War, many alien races suffered great defeats – but what fate befell the Gelth?

They were turned into _____

5 In my eighth incarnation, I refused to fight in the Time War, until I died crash-landing on the planet Karn. Who temporarily revived me?

The _____ of **Karn**

6 Which famous (or should that be infamous?) Time Lord was resurrected to lead the Time Lords in battle?

R _____

7 At the end of the war, I fought on a crucial battlefield, in a great Time Lord city on Gallifrey. What was that city called?

A _____

8 I thought I saw Davros's command ship destroyed during the first year of the Time War, when it flew into the jaws of which abomination?

The N_____ C_____

9 Who led the horrific Army of Meanwhiles and Never-weres during the war?

The C _____ H _____ B _____ K _____

10 At the end of the Time War, Gallifrey appeared to have been destroyed but was actually transported to an alternative dimension. Who was it that managed this incredible feat?

The _____

In the Moment

The timeline of the Last Great Time War is very confusing, considering it technically lasted for the entirety of eternity, but also ended when I made Gallifrey disappear. (Use the timey-wimey explanation if that helps you get your head around it.)

Can you un-muddle this muddled timeline of the events that happened at the end of the Time War? Simply put the following sentences into the correct order.

A Rather than destroy the Time Lords, all my incarnations set about freezing Gallifrey in one moment in time, then hide it away in a pocket universe.

B Having thwarted a Zygon invasion of Earth, we all return to Gallifrey on the last day of the Time War.

C The Moment manifests as Bad Wolf and tells me that I am to be the one to save the universe.

D The Moment opens a time fissure to show me the man I will become, and my tenth and eleventh incarnations pull the Warrior through the fissure to 16th-century England.

E My alter ego, the Warrior, steals the Moment from the Omega Arsenal.

F The Warrior, the man who regrets and the man who forgets all prepare to press the Big Red Button and activate the Moment.

A Sontaran Stratagem

The Sontarans and Rutans are ancient enemies, having been at war for more than 50,000 years. What they really need is a peacemaker.

Can you swap the three Sontaran 'S's with the three Rutan 'R's, in just fifteen moves? Each letter can only move into an empty space immediately next to it or jump over one other letter into an empty space.

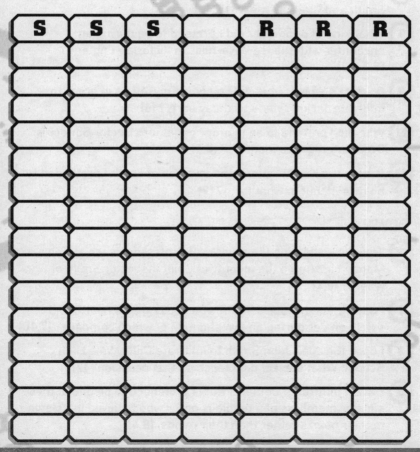

What's in a Name?

Hardly anyone knows my real name, but I've certainly gone by plenty of others over the years. Usually John Smith.

See how many of these questions you can answer about this and other mysterious alter egos of mine.

ACROSS

4 When I first met Mrs Gillyflower, I introduced myself as Doctor Smith and Clara as my what? **(4)**

7 What kind of puppeteer did I pretend to be during an encounter with the Ice Governess in Victorian England? **(5,3,4,3)**

9 On Pete's World, what did I disguise myself as in order to infiltrate Jackie Tyler's birthday party? **(6)**

11 Who did I pretend to be in order to get into Doctor Simeon's Great Intelligence Institute? **(8,6)**

12 During the Kraals' attempted invasion of Earth I pretended to be myself, but in what form? **(7)**

DOWN

1 While investigating the murder of Professor Peach at Eddison Manor, I assumed the identity of Chief Inspector Smith of where? **(8,4)**

2 I used the name John Smith when posing as a health and safety officer during an investigation of which company? **(7,10)**

3 I used the alias John Smith to infiltrate Deffry Vale High School. What subject did I teach on that occasion? **(7)**

5 Having infiltrated Demon's Run, I pretended to be one of these sinister members of a religious order who believed in listening to their hearts rather than their minds. **(8,4)**

6 I also used the alias John Smith when I went undercover at Coal Hill School, pretending to be the school's new what? **(9)**

8 I often referred to myself as John Smith when I was serving as scientific advisor to which military organisation? **(4)**

10 In 1913, I lived for a while as a schoolteacher called John Smith, but what subject did he teach? **(7)**

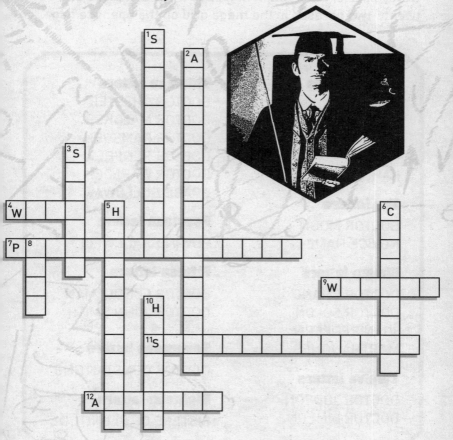

Doctor Who?

I have encountered scientists, medical experts, mad professors, healers and doctors of all varieties in my travels around the cosmos. Not all of them have been human, or even organic life forms.

You don't need a doctorate in etymology to work out this wordy puzzle, but it might help. See if you can place all twenty-two phrases in the mega grid on the opposite page.

Seven letters
HANDBOT
LIZ SHAW

Nine letters
KAHLER-JEX

Ten letters
DOCTOR MOON
NOVICE HAME

Eleven letters
DOCTOR CHANG
DOCTOR SOLON
JOAN REDFERN
MARTHA JONES

Twelve letters
DOCTOR JUDSON
DOCTOR SIMEON

Thirteen letters
DOCTOR CHESTER
DOCTOR MALOKEH
DOCTOR RAMSDEN
DOCTOR RENFREW
DOCTOR WARLOCK
GRACE HOLLOWAY

Fourteen letters
EDWIN BRACEWELL

Fifteen letters
DOCTOR FENDELMAN
DOCTOR JOHN SMITH

Seventeen letters
DOCTOR CONSTANTINE

Eighteen letters
SISTERS OF PLENITUDE

Prehistory Mystery

The Silurian race predates the dawn of human life on Earth, making them the original Earthlings. But how much do you know about *homo reptilia*? Fill in the blanks in the sentences below using the word bank. The words left over can be rearranged into a message of their own!

The Silurians went into _____ deep below the ground when an _____ was predicted.

Silurian society is divided into different _____: statesmen, scientists and _____ . There are different species of Silurians, too, including some with _____ eyes, and others that have venomous _____ .

The activities of humans have awoken sleeping Silurians on more than one occasion. In 1888, the construction of the _____ woke Madame Vastra and her sisters. Vastra became the Great _____ , who hunted down criminals and then ate them, including _____ .

Ark	Canada	apocalypse
as	classes	hibernation
three	as	warriors
London Underground	The	Silurian
	Jack the Ripper	Detective
tongues	wide	was

Who's Who?

Accessorise – that's the name of the game when you're busy saving the universe. If you've got something handy to hand like a sonic screwdriver you won't go far wrong. Although the sonic might be my favourite accessory, it's not the only one I've had over the centuries.

Can you match the items below to the incarnation of mine most associated with them?

Escape From the Forest

Your planet – the whole globe – becoming suddenly covered with forest in a matter of hours. What was all that about, eh? It was pretty weird to step out of the TARDIS in the middle of London and not be able to find my way around. It was a bit like being lost in a maze, only with added tigers.

Can you find your way out of the extreme maze on the next page, starting at the Natural History Museum and ending at the TARDIS?

START Natural History Museum

FINISH

The universe is an amazing place, full of all sorts of incredible life forms – animal, vegetable and mineral. You'd be astounded at how many plant-based races there are out there in your galaxy and beyond.

So, time for another puzzle. I have a selection of Androzani cones, Zolfa-Thuran cacti and Krynoid pods. The first two sets of scales balance. How many Krynoid pods are required to make the third set balance?

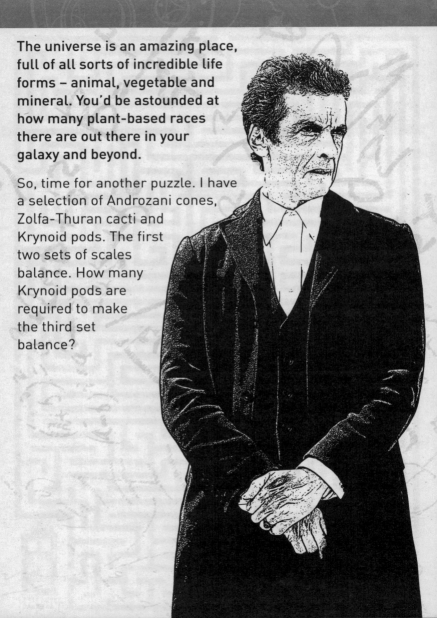

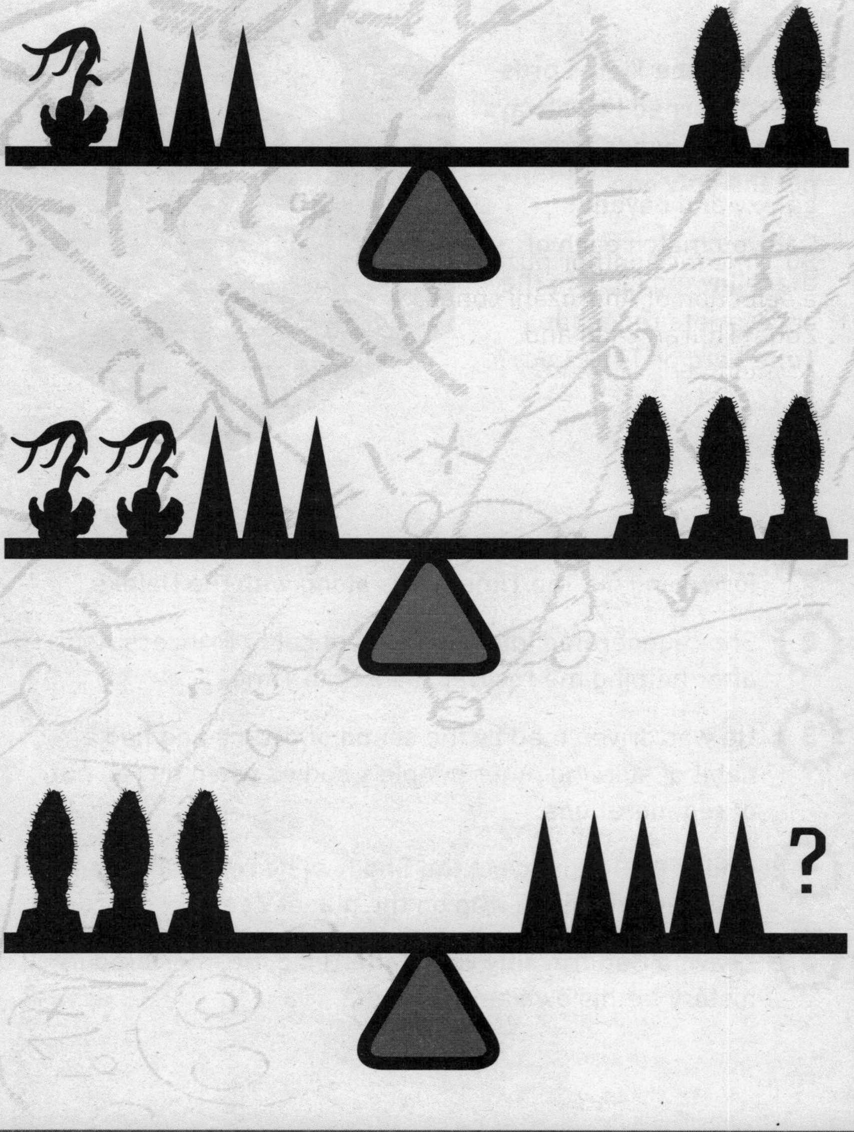

Renegades

As far as the Time Lords are concerned I've always been a renegade, but I'm not the only one.

Can you match each of the following facts to the appropriate renegade Time Lord or Time Lady?

1. For hundreds of years he believed he was responsible for wiping out the Time Lords along with the Daleks.

2. She regenerated into a form identical to Princess Astra after helping me recover the Key to Time.

3. He was driven mad by the sound of drums and had a habit of stealing other people's bodies when he ran out of regenerations.

4. Under the influence of the Shadow, he reluctantly led me and Romana into a trap on the planet Zeos.

5. Leaving Gallifrey fifty years after I did, he interfered in history for his own amusement.

6 Once called Magnus and a former friend of mine from my Academy days, he became a renegade, assisting the War Lords.

7 He had an Ouroboros snake tattoo in every regeneration and was one of the good ones – but had also been known to be bad on occasion.

8 She abducted eleven scientific geniuses from across time and space, including Albert Einstein, using their intellects to create a giant artificial brain.

9 In an attempt to escape from the anti-matter universe in which he had become trapped, he created a new body for himself using a biodata extract from my fifth incarnation.

10 Over 2,000 years old, an expert horse rider and able to disarm opponents using nothing more than a spoon.

A The Meddling Monk

B The Rani

C Omega

D The Corsair

E The Doctor

F Drax

G The Warrior

H The Master

I The War Chief

J Romana

The Master

Former friends, then enemies, and now . . . Now, I don't know what the Master (or rather Missy) and I are to each other, to be honest. But one thing I can be sure of is that she is still as bonkers as he ever was.

How much do you know about the most notorious and infamous Time Lord renegade of them all?

1 At the age of eight, the young Master gazed into the Time Vortex through the Untempered Schism. What happened to him as a result?

A   He went mad

B   One of his hearts failed

2 How did I defeat the Master when he brought the alien energy vampire Axos to Earth?

A   I trapped him in a time loop

B   I trapped him in the centre of the TARDIS

3 What did the Master pretend to be in order to form a coven and summon a Dæmon to the village of Devil's End?

A   A grocer

B   A vicar

4 One of the Master's favourite ways of killing people was to drastically shrink their bodies to the point where life functions ceased. What was the name of the weapon he used to achieve this?

A   Tissue Compression Eliminator

B   Flesh Crushing Destroyer

5 I once fought with the Master on Gallifrey and thought he had died after falling into a crevice. He had actually managed to gain access to his TARDIS, which was described as what?

A   A post box

B   A grandfather clock

6 Having run out of regenerations, whose body did the Master steal after becoming stranded on the planet Traken?

A   Tremas

B   The Rani

7 In England in 1215 the Master disguised himself as whom as part of an elaborate plan to stop King John from signing the Magna Carta?

A   Sir Gilles, a French knight

B   The Fifth Doctor

8 Having accidentally shrunk himself, what did the Master use to restore himself to a normal size on Sarn, the planet of fire?

A Volcanic lava

B Numismaton gas

9 What happened to the Master when he found himself on the semi-sentient Cheetah World?

A He destroyed all the Cheetah People

B He started to become a Cheetah Person

10 Fleeing the Last Great Time War, the Master travelled to the end of the universe and used a Chameleon Arch to turn himself into a human. What was the name of his human identity?

A Professor Yana

B Professor Wagg

11 Escaping to Earth in a new, younger incarnation – using my TARDIS, I might add – who did the Master become?

A Harold Saxon

B Henry Noone

12 What piece of alien technology did the Master use to turn the human race into the Master Race?

A The Chameleon Arch

B The Immortality Gate

Mirror, Mirror

Mirror, mirror, on the wall, who's the frowniest of them all? Oh, that'll be me. (As faces go, it's all right until you get to the attack eyebrows.)

Mirrors seem to exert a strange hold over humans, but they have a number of other unusual powers, from time travel to imprisoning aliens, too.

Take a look at these images of things in mirrors. Can you tell who or what it is that appears in each reflection?

4

5

6

7

8

Shakespeare Shmakespeare

William Shakespeare: show-off, potty-mouth and certifiable genius. I gave him all his best lines, you know. Which of the following lines are Shakespeare's and which are mine?

1 'Shall I compare thee to a summer's day?'

SHAKESPEARE · **THE DOCTOR**

2 'Fourteen lines, fourteen sides, fourteen facets. Oh, my head. Tetradecagon.'

SHAKESPEARE · **THE DOCTOR**

3 'Good mistress, this poor fellow has died from a sudden imbalance of the humours.'

SHAKESPEARE · **THE DOCTOR**

4 'There is nothing either good or bad, but thinking makes it so.'

SHAKESPEARE · **THE DOCTOR**

5 'Creature, I name you Carrionite!'

SHAKESPEARE · **THE DOCTOR**

6 'The fool doth think he is wise, but the wise man knows himself to be a fool.'

SHAKESPEARE · **THE DOCTOR**

7 'Oh, how to explain the mechanics of the infinite temporal flux?'

SHAKESPEARE   THE DOCTOR

8 'Good props store back there. I'm not sure about this though. Reminds me of a Sycorax.'

SHAKESPEARE   THE DOCTOR

9 'Lord, what fools these mortals be!'

SHAKESPEARE   THE DOCTOR

10 'Friends, Romans, countrymen, lend me your ears.'

SHAKESPEARE   THE DOCTOR

11 'Conscience is but a word that cowards use, devised at first to keep the strong in awe.'

SHAKESPEARE   THE DOCTOR

12 'Words of the right sound, the right shape, the right rhythm. Words that last forever.'

SHAKESPEARE   THE DOCTOR

13 'All the world's a stage.'

SHAKESPEARE   THE DOCTOR

Data Download

Missy – the Time Lord renegade formerly known as the Master – made an unwelcome reappearance after having followed my adventures for some time. It turned out she was the one who had brought Clara and me together in the first place (although we didn't know it at the time).

Missy travelled along my timeline, uploading the minds of the dying to the Nethersphere – a virtual reality housed within a Matrix data slice. Mad, I tell you. Completely bonkers, and then some!

Can you break the code on the opposite page by solving the Sudoku? It's almost as tricky to work out as Missy herself . . .

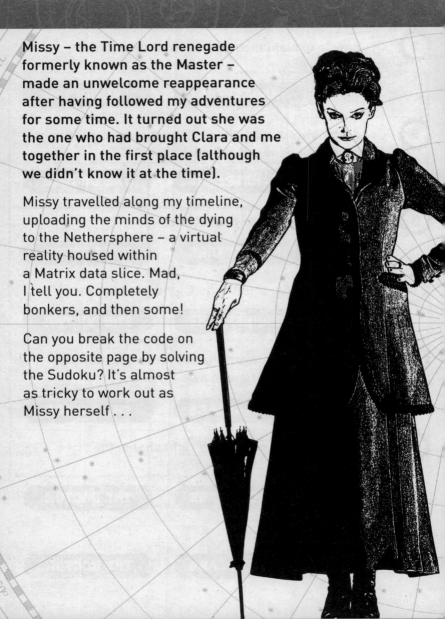

3		9	1		7	8		
	7		4	2		8	9		
		2	3			7	4	1
8	9	6		3				5
	7			2	4		9	8
	4			9	6	1	3	
9			4	1	2			6
4	2					3	7	9
	5	8	9	7			1	

Rise of the Cybermen

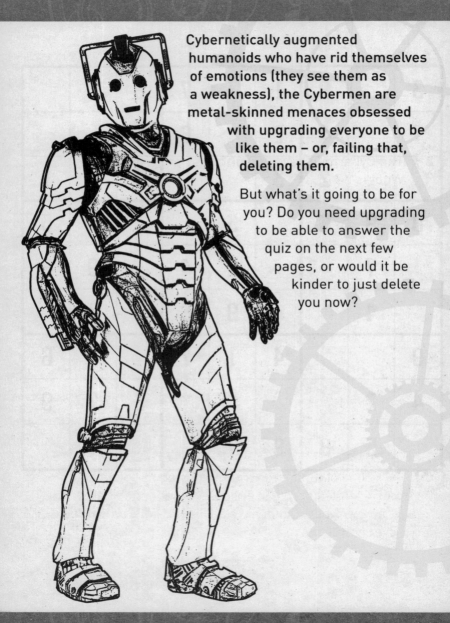

Cybernetically augmented humanoids who have rid themselves of emotions (they see them as a weakness), the Cybermen are metal-skinned menaces obsessed with upgrading everyone to be like them – or, failing that, deleting them.

But what's it going to be for you? Do you need upgrading to be able to answer the quiz on the next few pages, or would it be kinder to just delete you now?

1 I have encountered two different types of Cybermen. One type originated on Pete's World, but where in your universe did the other kind come from?

_____

2 The Cybermen have one priceless major weakness. What is it?

_____

3 The Cybermen share a consciousness similar to a hive mind, but what is it called?

_____

4 The Cybermen sometimes use small cyborgs as advance guards and energy thieves. What are they called?

_____

5 In 1988, a statue made from the living metal validium crash-landed on Earth and later went on to destroy an invading Cyberman fleet. What was the name of the silver statue?

_____

6 When the Cybermen tried to destroy Earth by crashing a space freighter into it in the 26th century, what extinction-level event did their actions actually result in?

_____

7 Which Davros-like figure was responsible for creating the Cybermen on Pete's World?

_____

8 Which of my other foes did the Cybermen clash with during the Battle of Canary Wharf?

_____

9 In 1851, a group of Cybus Cybermen threatened Victorian London with a CyberKing they had constructed under the Thames. What _is_ a CyberKing?

_____

10 Which Cyber faction monitored the area of space near Demon's Run in the 52nd century?

_____

11 Once home to the greatest theme park in the galaxy, which planet was the focus of another Cyberman uprising?

_____

12 Which masterful maniac brought the Cybermen back to Earth in 2014 in their millions?.

_____

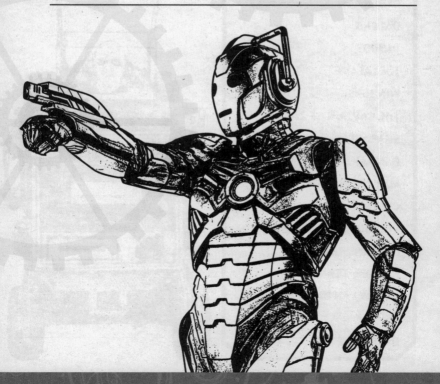

Cyborgs 101

If you've seen one cybernetic organism you've seen them all, believe me. They're a melding of flesh and metal greater than the sum of their parts, and usually lacking in some basic etiquette, like not trying to take over the universe every other Wednesday. I mean, that's just bad manners!

How many of the following machines – and in some cases alien biomechanoids – can you find hidden in this wordsearch?

THE DRAGON OF ICE WORLD

ICE WARRIORS

CYBERMEN

DALEKS

DAVROS

TOCLAFANE

WINDERS

THE CAPTAIN OF ZANAK

SKARASEN

BANNAKAFFALATTA

MAX CAPRICORN

CYBERSHADE

PEKING HOMUNCULUS

CASSANDRA O'BRIEN

KAHLER-TEK

TRICKY VAN BAALEN

PSI

DALEK PUPPET

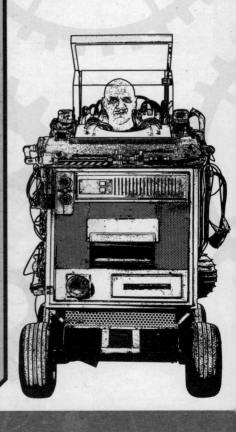

```
W X W G E R U N E E P S D S M C T H
N X O L D E R E D T E R E K A A A Z
H W A P A G V I K H K O E A X A X H
I L I G H N B R P E I I D R C F N K
O N I M S I M B N D N R D A A C L A
P S F D R L K O W R G R A S P E F N
P P L O E S E A M A H A L E R O C A
H M Y D B N N R P G O W E N I G K Z
I R V K Y U K D Q O M E K T C N W F
C A E T C G S N C N U C P F O I W O
N I B D A E O A K O N I U S R I Y N
N I U L H H R S N F C Y P D N C S I
R C B D L T V S J I U T P D D L L A
J V Y R Z K A A I C L O E F L S C T
T T N B W E D C A E U R T J R J R P
C Q S N E T N X N W S K E L A D N A
I D E T J R H D T O C L A F A N E C
W G B O L E M D R R F G R R R R H E
I O U T W L K E F L X I I O R O H H
C I G L H H B M N D V D Q L E N M T
A T T A L A F F A K A N N A B J E M
Z T R I C K Y V A N B A A L E N T R
```

Welcome to the Nethersphere

The virtual world created inside the Nethersphere by Missy
might have seemed like the real deal to those poor souls
stored within it, but it wasn't. And, as with any computer
system, sometimes glitches in the data would create a
slightly less than perfect copy of the real world.

Can you find ten differences (or glitches) between these two images of Missy and me outside St Paul's Cathedral?

Missy's Misdemeanours

Just like her former male incarnations, Missy has been responsible for a great deal of misery and mayhem. But surely among her worst crimes was the day she raised a Cyberarmy using Cyberpollen and the souls of the dead.

Can you put this list of events from that fateful day into the correct order?

A Missy gave me the coordinates to Gallifrey (although they turned out to be false).

B Freeing herself from her restraints, Missy disintegrated my friend from UNIT, Osgood.

C Missy teleported to the graveyard where I had landed my TARDIS.

D Missy met Clara and I at one of 3W's mausoleums, hidden inside St Paul's Cathedral.

E Missy was captured by UNIT and taken on to Boat One, UNIT's presidential aeroplane.

F Missy was shot by a rogue Cyberman.

G As the Cybermen destroyed the plane, Missy teleported away.

H Missy gave me control of her Cyberman army, hoping to prove how similar we were.

I Missy kissed me and then revealed her true identity.

J Missy signalled the Cybermen, who then attacked the plane.

Mistress of Mayhem

Missy is a menace all the time, but never more so than when she's waving her multi-purpose device around. From vaporising her enemies to taking selfies, there seemed to be no end to the tricks she could play with it.

Can you crack this code to deactivate Missy's device?

Using the digits **1** to **7** only once each, put one number in each circle so that each line adds up to the same total.

Ghosts of Christmas Past

Christmas: a time to get together with friends and family, eat overcooked turkey and argue about games of Monopoly. Or, in my case, save the Earth from conquering alien hordes. What could be more traditional than that?

So, how much attention have you been paying at Christmas? Have you spotted any robots disguised as Santa Claus, for example? Or did you see the *Titanic* zoom over the roof of Buckingham Palace that one time?

 1 When the Sycorax attempted to invade Earth on Christmas Day, what did they use to hypnotise a third of the population of the planet?

_____

 2 When I first met Donna Noble, on her supposed wedding day at Christmas time, she called me an alien from which planet?

_____

3 Who was the owner of the spaceship replica of the *Titanic* that almost crashed on London on Christmas Day in 2008?

_____

4 Landing in London on Christmas Eve 1851, I promptly ran into a man who believed himself to be me – plus his companion Rosita, and which cyborganic creature?

_____

5 Who allied herself with the Cybermen trapped in Victorian London, and ultimately became the CyberKing?

_____

_____

6 Another Christmas Day saw not only the human race become the Master Race, but also the return of which race thought lost to the Last Great Time War?

_____

7 Which frosty maiden did the miserly Kazran Sardick spend time with every Christmas Eve, the two of them having fallen in love?

_____

_____

8 Who came to my aid after I fell to Earth on Christmas Eve in 1938?

_____

_____

9 In 1892, which of my enduring enemies created the Ice Governess using telepathic snow?

_____

_____

10 What surrounded the town of Christmas, making it so that no one could lie?

_____

11 At a base in the North Pole one Christmas, Santa Claus helped Clara and me defeat the Kantrofarri. But what are the Kantrofarri more commonly known as?

_____

12 Which alien species attempted to possess the body of every human being on Earth on Christmas Eve in 1869?

_____

I Am the Doctor

I have lived for over 2,000 years and in that time I have had quite a few adventures. As to what lies ahead, only time will tell. My past escapades have been thoroughly documented, though, so you should know me pretty well by now. How many of these questions can you answer about this enigmatic alien time traveller?

1 In my **first** incarnation I had a fondness for hypnotising people, but what did I use to help me achieve this feat?

_____

2 My **second** incarnation was put on trial by the Time Lords for interfering in galactic affairs. Having been found guilty, what was my punishment?

_____

_____

_____

3 My **third** incarnation had a fondness for gadgets and fast cars, but what type of vehicle was the Whomobile?

_____

 4 In my **fourth** incarnation I liked to carry a yo-yo with me. I put it to good use on the Nerva Beacon space station (also known as The Ark) but for what purpose?

_____

_____

_____

 5 My **fifth** incarnation had a particular talent for which sport?

_____

6 In my **sixth** incarnation, as well as a rather garish coat and stripy yellow trousers, I liked to wear a brooch, but what animal was it in the shape of?

_____

7 I've always enjoyed a little sleight of hand, but in my **seventh** incarnation I took my skills to a new level. I was also a master chess-player and liked to play which 'musical instrument'?

_____

8 I've always demonstrated a flair for fashion (at least most of my incarnations have). Upon regenerating into my **eighth** incarnation, where did I get my smart 19th-century outfit from?

9 What was it that finished off my **ninth** incarnation, forcing my body to regenerate once again?

_____

_____

10 When I encountered the Master for the first time during my **tenth** incarnation, he aged my body so that it looked as it would if I had lived for over 900 years without regenerating. What device did he use to accomplish this?

_____

11 My **eleventh** incarnation demonstrated a natural ability for which team sport?

_____

12 In my **twelfth** incarnation as the Doctor, what did I call the device I invented to return flattened objects to their original 3D state and that I used to defeat the Boneless?

_____

13 I've not always gone by the name 'the Doctor'. In the guise of **a warrior** during the Time War, I earned a title by which the Daleks would come to know me for all the centuries to follow. What was it?

_____

Answers

PART 1: NEWLY REGENERATED

The Regeneration Game
pages 14–15

'Shoes. Must find my shoes.'
Third Doctor

'Typical Sontaran attitude . . . stop
Linx . . . perverting the course of
human history . . .'
Fourth Doctor

'Kidneys! I've got new kidneys! I don't
like the colour.'
Twelfth Doctor

'Slower! Slower! Concentrate on one
thing. One thing!'
Second Doctor

'Legs! Still got legs, good!!
Arms, hands. Ooh, fingers. Lots
of fingers.'
Eleventh Doctor

'You were expecting someone else?'
Sixth Doctor

'Who am I? Who am I?'
Eighth Doctor

'Oh no, Mel.'
Seventh Doctor

'Hello! OK – oh. New teeth. That's
weird. So, where was I? Oh, that's
right. Barcelona!'
Tenth Doctor

'I . . . Oh . . .'
Fifth Doctor

Trenzalore Test
pages 16–19
1) a 2) b 3) c 4) b 5) c 6) c

7) a 8) a 9) b 10) c 11) c
12) b 13) a

The Game is Afoot
page 20

Paternoster Irregular	Half-Face Man	T-Rex	Sonic Shield
Sonic Shield	T-Rex	Half-Face Man	Paternoster Irregular
T-Rex	Paternoster Irregular	Sonic Shield	Half-Face Man
Half-Face Man	Sonic Shield	Paternoster Irregular	T-Rex

Puzzling Pairs
page 21
Clara (D)

Alien Alliance
pages 22–23

```
H R S J H J O S C N W G U N H
U S A Y N O N W A E E D U G A
F U I D C I I T B M E A V O E
Q R O F V O R X T R V B V D M
R V O H W A R Q I E I U P U O
J D A I X O V A S B L T L J G
X R R I D D L I X Y S W H N O
J S D A W V L B W C N G J O T
S X B G C U S L I T H E E N H
C K U D R O S N A R A T N O S
C P E I M S N O T U A W T J N
Y H A L T E R L L E P T I L S
T N K B A O E Q A Z Y G O N S
S G Q G S D E P N N V S S Z H
B S H U P I Y I M G S V Y E B
```

The TARDIS –
A Beginner's Guide
pages 24–27
1) Time And Relative Dimension in
Space
2) Type 40 TT Capsule
3) The Chameleon Circuit

4) Wood
5) Six
6) The Time Rotor
7) A hatstand
8) The SS Titanic
9) In the swimming pool, which happened to be in the library at the time, so either answer is correct
10) Idris

The Paternoster Gang
pages 28–29
In the order they appear in the text: Paternoster Row, Silurian, Demons Run, Great Intelligence, snow, Crimson Horror, Sweetville, Red Leech, Trenzalore.

Repurpose, Repair, Repeat
pages 30–31
1) d 2) b 3) c 4) a

Into the Dalek
pages 32–33

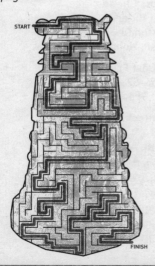

Dalek Deductions
pages 34–35
1) f 2) j 3) h 4) i 5) g 6) c
7) e 8) a 9) d 10) b

Alien Museum
page 36

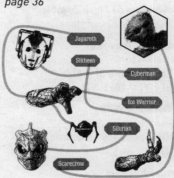

Escape From the Pandorica
page 37

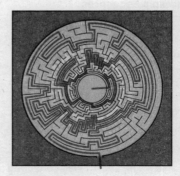

Deadly Dinosaurs
pages 38–39
ACROSS – 2) T Rex 4) Triceratops
6) Velociraptors
DOWN – 1) T Rex 2) Triceratops
3) Stegosaurus 5) Pterodactyl

The Impossible Girl
pages 40–41
ACROSS – 4) Teacher
6) Remember **9)** Dalek Asylum
10) Smaller
DOWN – 1) Timeline **2)** Leaf
3) Governess **5)** Time Zombie
7) Danny Pink **8)** Cumbria

The Lonely Traveller
pages 42–45
1) c 2) c 3) a 4) a 5) b 6) b
7) a 8) c 9) b 10) b 11) a 12) c

The Doctor's Wife
page 46
'**TARDIS**' appears nine times and
'**IDRIS**' appears ten times

Unusual Entities
page 47
1) b 2) b 3) c

Spaceship Sequences
pages 48–49
1) c 2) d 3) e 4) a 5) d

Riddles of Sherwood
pages 50–51
1) True
2) True
3) False – We realised the sheriff's
knights were robots when one of
them got its arm cut off
4) True
5) False – The sheriff was collecting
all the gold in the region to repair
the damaged ship
6) False – The ship originated from
the 29th century
7) False – Robin fired the arrow into
the ship's engines to make sure

that it did leave Earth's atmosphere
before blowing up
8) True

Know Your Robot
pages 52–53
1) Mummy Servitor Robot
2) Roboform
3) Clockwork Droid
4) Dr Edwin Bracewell
5) K-9
6) Smiler
7) Gadget
8) The Heavenly Host

Famous Faces
pages 54–55
1) Queen Nefertiti
2) William Shakespeare
3) Madame de Pompadour
4) Charles Dickens
5) Queen Victoria
6) Vincent van Gogh
7) Agatha Christie
8) Adolf Hitler
9) Winston Churchill
10) Robin Hood

Man's Best Friend
pages 56–57
1) d 2) f 3) a 4) e 5) b 6) c

Alien Attack!
page 58
Minotaur, Auton, Carrionite,
Racnoss, Adipose = **MACRA**

3D or Not 3D
page 59
1) Not 3D
2) 3D
3) Not 3D

4) 3D
5) Not 3D

Airlock Logic
pages 60–61

1) LOCK
SOCK
SICK
SINK

2) SINK
SINS
SONS
DONS

3) DONS
DOES
DYES
EYES

4) EYES
EVES
EVEN
OVEN
OPEN

Time Lord Trials
pages 62–63
Home – Gallifrey
The Ultimate Enemy – the Daleks
Behind Every Great Man – Missy
A Sort of Physician – the Doctor

Do You Speak Gallifreyan?
pages 64–65
GALLIFREY FALLS NO MORE

Don't Blink!
pages 66–67

PART 2: DECENT DOCTOR

Biological Brain-teasers
pages 70–71
1) two 2) four 3) twelve 4) ten
5) six 6) eight 7) five 8) three
The total is 50

The Sonic
pages 72–73

SONICSCREWDRIVER
ULTRASONIC
SONICLANCE
SONICPEN
SONICLIPSTICK
SONICCLIPSTICK
SONICCANE
SONICKNIFE
SONICRAYGUN
SONICGUN
SONICPROBE
SONICCONE
SONICDOORHANDLE
SONICBLASTER

Don't Tell
pages 74–75

Journey to the Centre of the TARDIS
pages 76–77
1) Dimensionally Transcendental
2) Rassilon Imprimatur
3) Ancillary Power Station
4) St John Ambulance
5) Cloister Room
6) State of Decay
7) Artron Energy
8) Time Vortex

An Awful Lot of Running
pages 78–81
1) b 2) a 3) c 4) c 5) c 6) b
7) a 8) c 9) b 10) a 11) b 12) a

TARDIS Transformations
pages 82–83
1) f 2) e 3) c 4) b 5) d 6) a

Memory Worm Mysteries
pages 84–85
1) Liz Ten – aka Queen Elizabeth the Tenth
2) Kahler-Tek
3) Martha Jones
4) Henry Avery
5) Jenny
6) Craig Owens
7) Kate Stewart
8) Jackson Lake
9) Emperor Ludens Nimrod Kendrick Cord Longstaff XLI – aka Porridge
10) Wilfred Mott

Alien A to Z
pages 86–91
A – Adipose
B – Boneless
C – Carrionites
D – Daleks
E – Eknodines
F – Fendahleen
G – Gelth
H – Hath
I – Ice Warriors
J – Judoon
K – Krafayis
L – Logopolitans
M – Macra
N – Nimon
O – Ogri
P – Pyroviles
R – Raxacoricofallapatorians
S – Saturnynes
T – Tetraps
U – Urbankans
V – Vashta Nerada
W – Whisper Men
XYZ – Zygons

Take Care
page 92

	SCHOOL HALL			CARETAKER'S WORKSHOP		
	2	1	5	3	6	4
	4	6	3	1	2	5
ENGLISH CLASSROOM	1	3	6	5	4	2	MATHS CLASSROOM
	5	2	4	6	3	1
	3	5	2	4	1	6
	6	4	1	2	5	3
	STAFFROOM			DINING HALL		

School's Out!
page 93
1) KRILLITANES
2) THE FAMILY OF BLOOD
3) DALEKS
4) SLITHEEN
5) SKOVOX BLITZER

Coal Hill Conundrums
pages 94–95
1) Shoreditch in East London
2) I was her grandfather
3) History
4) Ian Chesterton
5) Headmaster
6) Hand of Omega
7) Baseball bat
8) Courtney Woods
9) The Cadet Squad
10) It's quiet at night

In the Pink
page 96
ACROSS – 3) Sergeant
4) Mathematics 6) Rupert
7) Gloucester 8) Nethersphere
DOWN – 1) Afghanistan
2) Dream Crab 5) Skovox Blitzer

Noble Sacrifice
page 97
1) Danny Pink
2) Adric
3) Astrid Peth
4) Amy Pond
5) Mickey Smith
6) Donna Noble

What's in the Wi-Fi?
pages 98–99

1)
MONK
MOCK
MUCK
BUCK
BULK
BULL
BELL
HELL
HELP

2)
TABLET
TABLES
CABLES
CABLED
CALLED
CALKED
TALKED
TACKED
HACKED

3)
SPOON
SWOON
SWORN
SWORE
STORE
STARE
STARS
SEARS
HEARS
HEADS

Kill the Moon
pages 100–101
Piece A

Moon Mysteries
pages 102–103
1) A Dalek flying saucer
2) The Silence
3) The Cybermen
4) The Judoon
5) Germs
6) River Song
7) Five
8) Torchwood House
9) Doctor Moon
10) Inside the Medusa Cascade

Lost Worlds
page 104

Cascade Coordinates
page 105

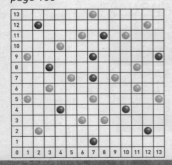

Arachnophobia
pages 106–107

In Case of Emergency
pages 108–111
1) a) Hostile Action Displacement System
2) b) The Cloister Bell
3) a) The Fast Return Switch
4) True
5) c) The Chameleon Arch
6) a) TARDIS keys
7) True
8) c) Big Friendly Button
9) a) Siege Mode
10) True
11) b) Emergency Program One returns a companion to a safe place, away from danger

The Sands of Time
pages 112–113
Blank face 1: should show 5:24
Blank face 2: should show 8:42
Blank face 3: should show 12:00
The clocks are going forward by 66 minutes

How Great Is Your Intelligence?
pages 114–115
1) True
2) False – Simeon was turned into an ice-faced zombie
3) True
4) False – The Great Intelligence was hiding in the Wi-Fi
5) False – Miss Kizlet was working for the Great Intelligence
6) True
7) False – The Great Intelligence once tried to take over London's underground railway system
8) True
9) True
10) False – Jenny Flint called the Great Intelligence 'a mind without a body'

Brave Hearts
pages 116–119
1) Susan Foreman
2) Sarah Jane Smith
3) Leela
4) Tegan Jovanka
5) Dr Grace Holloway
6) Rose Tyler
7) Madame de Pompadour
8) Astrid Peth
9) Queen Elizabeth I
10) Sally Sparrow
11) Marilyn Monroe
12) Lady Christina de Souza
13) Joan Redfern
14) River Song
15) Clara Oswald

Child of the TARDIS
page 120
1) Demons Run

2) Mels
3) Me – the Doctor!
4) Melody Pond
5) Vortex Manipulator
6) TARDIS
7) Library

Hello, Sweetie
page 121
1) e 2) c 3) a 4) d 5) b

Timey-Wimey Crossword
pages 122–123
ACROSS – 3) Atomic Clock
6) Big Ben 7) Grandfather Clock
8) Clock Tower
DOWN – 1) Sundial
2) Clockwork Droids
4) Invisibility Watch
5) Fob Watch

PART 3: TRUE TIME LORD

Spoilers!
page 126–127
1) True
2) False – The Moment took the form of Rose Tyler (or Bad Wolf, if you prefer)
3) True
4) True
5) False – I was travelling with Martha Jones at the time
6) True
7) False – I did say this, but not in my first incarnation
8) True

Flatlined
pages 128–129
Net 2

Hiding in the Shadows
pages 130–131
1) Auton
2) Catkind
3) Ice Warrior
4) Ood
5) Slitheen
6) Pyrovile
7) Zygon
8) Dalek
9) Cyberman
10) Foretold

The Bells
pages 132–133
1) a 2) b 3) b 4) c 5) c 6) a 7) a

No Entry
page 134
EXIT STRATEGY

Trouble[3]
page 135
1) The Pandorica
2) Shakri cube
3) Rubik's cube
4) The TARDIS in siege mode
5) Hypercube
6) Stasis cube

Time War History
page 136–137
1) Ten million
2) The Time Vaults on Gallifrey
3) The Moment
4) They were turned into gas
5) The Sisterhood of Karn
6) Rassilon
7) Arcadia
8) The Nightmare Child
9) The Could Have Been King

10) Me, of course – all thirteen incarnations of the Doctor!

In the Moment
page 138
E C D B F A

A Sontaran Stratagem
page 139

START						
S	S	S		R	R	R
S	S		S	R	R	R
S	S	R	S		R	R
S	S	R	S	R		R
S	S	R		R	S	R
S		R	S	R	S	R
	S	R	S	R	S	R
R	S	R	S	R		R
R	S	R	S		S	R
R	S	R	S	R	S	
R	S	R	S	R		S
R	S	R		R	S	S
R		R	S	R	S	S
R	R		S	R	S	S
R	R	R	S		S	S
R	R	R		S	S	S

What's in a Name?
pages 140–141
ACROSS - **4)** Wife **7)** Punch and Judy Man **9)** Waiter **11)** Sherlock Holmes **12)** Android
DOWN - **1)** Scotland Yard **2)** Adipose Industries **3)** Science **5)** Headless Monk **6)** Caretaker **8)** UNIT **10)** History

Doctor Who?
pages 142–143
ACROSS - **1)** Doctor Warlock **2)** Doctor Fendelman **6)** Doctor Moon **9)** Kahler-Jex **11)** Grace Holloway **15)** Sisters of Plenitude

18) Doctor Chang 19) Doctor Renfrew 20) Joan Redfern 21) Doctor Chester
DOWN - 1) Doctor John Smith 3) Edwin Bracewell 4) Handbot 5) Martha Jones 7) Doctor Malokeh 8) Doctor Solon 10) Doctor Constantine 12) Doctor Judson 13) Liz Shaw 14) Doctor Ramsden 16) Doctor Simeon 17) Novice Hame

Prehistory Mystery
page 144
In the order they appear in the text: hibernation, apocalypse, classes, warriors, three, tongues, London Underground, Detective, Jack the Ripper

Hidden message: The Silurian Ark was as wide as Canada

Who's Who?
page 145
1) Umbrella – **Seventh**
2) Jelly babies – **Fourth**, although my **Eighth** incarnation was also partial
3) Fez – **Eleventh**
4) Stick of celery – **Fifth**
5) Recorder – **Second**
6) 3D specs – **Tenth**
7) Bessie – **Third**
8) Scarf – **Fourth**

Escape From the Forest
page 146–147

How Does Your Garden Grow?
pages 148–149
Four Krynoid pods are required to balance the third set of scales

Renegades
pages 150–151
1) g 2) j 3) h 4) f 5) a 6) i
7) d 8) b 9) c 10) e

The Master
pages 152–155
1) **A** - He went mad
2) **A** - I trapped him in a time loop
3) **B** - Mr Magister, the local vicar
4) **A** - Tissue Compression Eliminator
5) **B** - A grandfather clock
6) **A** - Tremas

7) A - Sir Gilles, a French knight
8) B - Numismaton gas
9) B - He began to turn into a Cheetah Person himself
10) A - Professor Yana
11) A - Harold Saxon, Prime Minister of Great Britain
12) B - The Immortality Gate, a Vinvocci medical machine

Mirror, Mirror
pages 156–157
1) Sister of Mine
2) The Mara
3) The Krafayis
4) The TARDIS
5) Sarah Jane
6) Zygon
7) Scaroth, last of the Jagaroth
8) Donna Noble

Shakespeare Shmakespeare
pages 158–159
1) Shakespeare
2) The Doctor
3) The Doctor
4) Shakespeare
5) The Doctor
6) Shakespeare
7) The Doctor
8) The Doctor
9) Shakespeare
10) Shakespeare
11) Shakespeare
12) The Doctor
13) Both Shakespeare and the Doctor

Data Download
pages 160–161

3	6	9	1	4	7	8	5	2
7	1	4	2	5	8	9	6	3
5	8	2	3	6	9	7	4	1
8	9	6	7	3	1	4	2	5
1	7	3	5	2	4	6	9	8
2	4	5	8	9	6	1	3	7
9	3	7	4	1	2	5	8	6
4	2	1	6	8	5	3	7	9
6	5	8	9	7	3	2	1	4

Rise of the Cybermen
pages 162–165
1) Earth's former twin planet, Mondas
2) Gold
3) The Cyberiad
4) Cybermats
5) Nemesis
6) The destruction of the dinosaurs (or at least most of them)
7) John Lumic, owner of Cybus Industries
8) The Daleks
9) A Dreadnought-class ship, used to cripple whole cities and upgrade their populations
10) The Twelfth Cyber Legion
11) Hedgewick's World of Wonders
12) Missy, formerly known as the Master

Cyborgs 101
pages 166–167

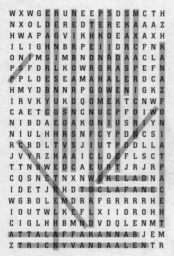

```
W X W G E R U N E E P S D S M C T H
N X O L D E R E D T E R E K A A A Z
H W A P A G V I K H K O E A X A X H
I L I G H N B R P E I I D R C F N K
O N I M S I M B N D N R D A A C L A
P S F D R L K O W R G R A S P E F N
P P L O E S E A M A H A L E R O C A
H M Y D B N N R P G O W E N I G K Z
I R V K Y U K D Q O M E K T C N W F
C A E T C G S N C N U C P F O I W O
N I B D A E O A K O N I U S R I Y N
N I U L H H R S N F C Y P D N C S I
R C B D L T V S J I U T P D D L L A
J V Y R Z K A A I C L O E F L S C T
T T N B W E D C A E U R T J R J R P
C Q S N E T N X N W S K E L A D N A
I D E T J R H D T O C L A F A N E C
W G B O L E M D R R F G R R R R H E
I O U T W L K E F L X I I O R O H H
C I G L H H B M N D V D Q L E N M T
A T T A L A F F A K A N N A B J E M
Z T R I C K Y V A N B A A L E N T R
```

Welcome to the Nethersphere
pages 168–169

Missy's Misdemeanours
page 170

D, I, E, J, B, G, C, H, A, F

Mistress of Mayhem
page 171

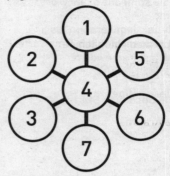

Ghosts of Christmas Past
pages 172–175
1) Blood Control
2) Mars
3) Max Capricorn
4) A Cybershade
5) Miss Mercy Hartigan
6) The Time Lords
7) Abigail Pettigrew
8) Madge Arwell
9) The Great Intelligence
10) A truth field
11) Dream Crabs
12) The Gelth

I Am the Doctor
pages 176–179
1) My signet ring
2) Forced to regenerate and live in exile on Earth

3) A hovercraft
4) To test the local gravity
5) Cricket
6) A cat
7) The spoons
8) I stole someone's fancy-dress costume
9) Cellular degeneration (as a result of absorbing the Time Vortex)
10) His laser screwdriver
11) Football
12) The 2Dis
13) The Oncoming Storm